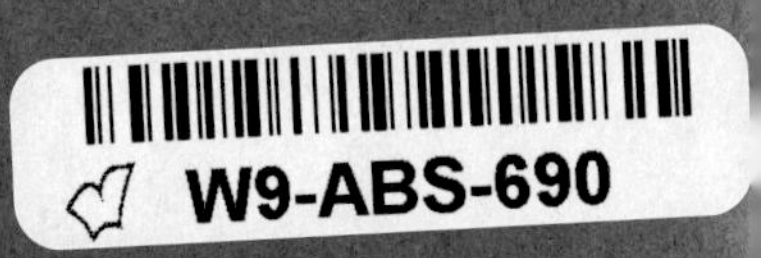
W9-ABS-690

Desperate Games

Other Books by Pierre Boulle

The Bridge over the River Kwai
Planet of the Apes
Ears of the Jungle
Garden on the Moon
Because It Is Absurd
My Own River Kwai
The Photographer
Time Out of Mind
The Executioner
A Noble Profession
S.O.P.H.I.A.
The Other Side of the Coin
The Test
Face of a Hero
Not the Glory

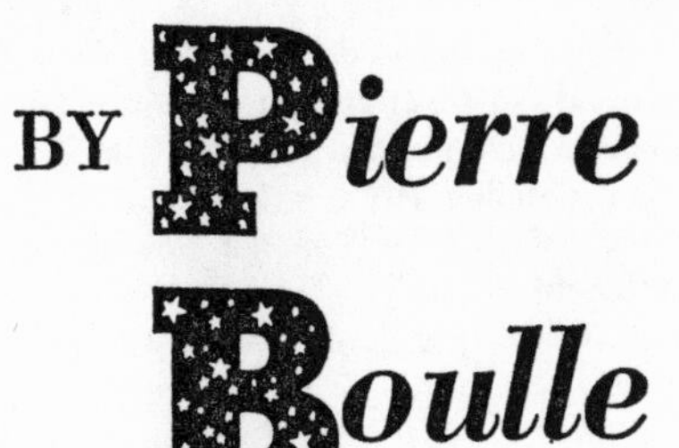

Translation by Patricia Wolf

The Vanguard Press, Inc. New York

 Manufactured in the United States of America.
Designer: Ernst Reichl
Library of Congress Catalogue Card Number: 73-83035
SBN 8149-0731-8

I am among those
who think well of the human character
generally.

Thomas Jefferson

1

A BELL RANG. The candidates, who had been waiting half an hour making polite, strained conversation to calm their nerves, fell silent. Though normally self-possessed, they all had felt the same anxiety, the same tension. The Institute's massive door was opened by an usher in formal attire. They followed him along a dim corridor into the main amphitheater where the final examinations were to be held. There were thirteen of them, ranging in age from thirty-five to fifty.

Fawell was among the first to enter the hall. Like the others, he brought no papers or calculating devices. Logarithmic tables, even ordinary slide rules, were forbidden. In this final exam they were expected to rely entirely on memory, knowledge, intelligence, and imagination.

This examination — actually a contest designed to select the best of the thirteen — was the last stage of an important intelligence-measuring operation that had been going on for more than three months and involved an impressive series of tests, some of which were eliminative.

The candidates — numerous at the beginning — had found themselves dealing with a succession of problems in higher mathematics, theoretical and experimental physics, chemistry, astronomy, astrophysics, cosmology, and matters embracing the various biological sciences; in short, an imposing array of subjects demanding thorough knowledge of the noblest and most diverse realms of human endeavor.

As the intelligence level was very high (all were graduates of world-renowned universities and many already had made their marks with important research or original theory), the tests had bristled with difficulties, requiring mastery of complex problems as well as a good measure of independent thinking, with the result that these essays were equivalent to doctoral theses. At this stage the participants had been allowed to use tables and calculators in addition to the Institute's computers and its library containing nearly the full range of human knowledge. Cramming was out of the question, for the examination had aimed at evaluating broad scientific learning; the topics had been set by a committee of undisputed international authorities, known as "Nobels" because they were all recipients of that award's supreme sanction.

During the three long months of preliminary tests, the candidates had been cloistered in the Institute, free to use its laboratories, computers, and library, but cut off from the outside world and lodged in monkish cells specially arranged for the occasion.

The examiners were also Nobels. No one else could have handled their task in view of the transcendent topics they had assigned. They had judged severely, mindful of their sober responsibility. The several thousand initial applicants had found their ranks gradually thinning. The three preliminary essays in mathematics, theoretical physics, and chemistry had at once narrowed the field: any candidate receiving a grade of less than eighty was rejected. Thus the majority had become rejects. The hundred or so remaining took the next set of tests and finally were allowed outside the Institute while the Nobel panel in turn closeted itself to deliberate.

The result of their discussions had been published a few days before. Only thirteen persons had managed to qualify. That was apparent at the start of the finals: there were only thirteen places. Fawell was among the chosen.

He went to his assigned place, as did his companions. They all sat down, waiting silently for the distribution of envelopes containing the exam questions.

The amphitheater, capable of holding a thousand, looked strangely empty. The thirteen survivors were seated as far as possible from one another — not to discourage cribbing (the nature of the finals made such maneuvers futile; besides, no one doubted the candidates' honesty), but to help them concentrate. Actually, Fawell felt this isolation as an uncomfortable weight on his shoulders. In spite of the countless exams he had taken and survived brilliantly in the past, the rush of fear now invading him was something he had not experienced since youth. He scrutinized his companions for signs of the same discomfort.

The two closest were old friends: Yranne and Mrs. Betty Han. They had been to college together and kept in touch afterwards. Yranne was a French mathematician who made frequent trips to the United States. Fawell, an American himself, called on him from time to time for help with certain calculations involved in his own research. He admired Yranne's logical mind and deductive powers.

Fawell's specialty was nuclear physics. After graduation he had trained under one of the greatest experts, the Nobel O'Kearn; later, on his own, he gained a reputation in academic circles for some interesting discoveries on antiparticles. Like Yranne, he was just over forty, the average age for this competition. A ruling restricted the age of candidates to between thirty-five and fifty. The duties which the thirteen finalists, and chiefly the winner, would be expected to perform were as incompatible with extreme youth as with the sclerosis of advanced age.

Mrs. Han (Betty to her friends) had a seat on one of the lower tiers. The fact that she was the only woman finalist had prompted a number of innuendos from women previously eliminated. But theirs were lone voices; the Nobel panel's scrupulous objectivity was generally taken for granted. Fawell felt glad and surprised to see her after fearing that she had been weeded out. She was brilliant beyond a doubt, but math and physics were not her field. She had started out to do serious scientific work and had given it up, despite outstanding marks, in order to explore disciplines frowned upon as frivolous by certain scholars. That was how she became fascinated with literature, only to branch into philosophy, and finally psychology in which she majored. She had won all kinds of honors in the field, yet former fellow-students teased her about such decadence. The fact that she had passed the exams in pure science which specialists had failed was fresh evidence of her intellectual prowess; of her powers of concentration as well, for she had relearned forgotten material in the few weeks preceding the competition.

Fawell, having advised her, welcomed her success; he was not one to disparage psychology and thought it a good thing that Betty was among the thirteen. To his congratulations she had replied with a grin that her psychology major had proved useful even in a math exam, having inspired a line of approach guaranteed to win the heart of a Nobel board. Betty, a Chinese separated for some time from her American husband, had retained her own nationality, an accepted status since relations became normalized between the two countries. This in no way altered her ties with the American scientific community. In the intellectual circles frequented by men like Fawell or Yranne, questions of nationality, race, and religion had long ago ceased to have any meaning.

Fawell, father of an eighteen-year-old daughter, had no objection to Ruth's marrying a Russian, as she planned to do. Her sweetheart, the son of a well-known astronomer, was Nicholas Zarratoff, whom she had met while accompanying her father to the Soviet Union for a scientific conference. The physicist would have preferred some young scholar for a son-in-law; still, Nicholas seemed an acceptable match. At twenty-six, he had already made a career for himself in aviation, and now that he had recently branched into astronautics, he could look forward to an even better one. Besides, his father was a friend of Fawell, who ardently admired the astronomer's almost mystical passion for science. The parents had not opposed the marriage, but as Ruth was still rather young, they asked the couple to wait and think it over for a year or so.

The elder Zarratoff was also there in the amphitheater. Glancing over his shoulder, Fawell saw him sitting in the top row. He smiled, musing that fate surely had destined the astronomer for the seat nearest the sky, his habitat. It was not surprising to find this Russian among the thirteen finalists; an expert in his field, he possessed vast scientific knowledge as well as a fertile imagination.

Yranne was like that too; he enjoyed toying with intricate problems.

How remarkable that all four of us were chosen, the physicist thought contentedly: Betty, Yranne, Zarratoff, and myself. Success did not bewilder Fawell, secure in the knowledge of his own worth, and confident that his keen mind was a match for the best brains of his generation.

The other finalists were less familiar to him. They included two biologists, a chemist, and a majority of fellow-physicists. But this was no time for reading faces. Fawell shifted his gaze to the front of the hall, to the imposing platform onto which the usher was conducting three members of the examining board — three Nobels.

2

THE THREE EMINENT scientists also wore formal attire. First came O'Kearn himself, celebrated dean of Nobels, in whose laboratory Fawell had worked for many years. His majestic bearing matched his reputation; glowing eyes peered out with singular luster from a face deeply furrowed by study and passionate research. A halo of unruly white hair vaguely recalled certain portraits of Einstein; he was apt to try to accentuate the resemblance by studiously cultivating this tousled look.

As the examiners walked in, the thirteen candidates exchanged furtive glances, then rose in a body, a custom observed long ago in certain universities at the entrance of a famous scholar. Fawell couldn't help smiling when he recognized this holdover from his student days. The three scientists seemed flattered, and O'Kearn motioned to the examinees to sit down. He raised an envelope above his head.

"Madam, gentlemen," he began, "here are the topics. I declare . . . we — my two colleagues and I — declare that the envelope's seal is unbroken, as you can probably tell from where you sit. However," he added with a grin, "anyone with the slightest doubt may step up and verify it."

A murmur of polite protest greeted the jest; not for a minute did anyone question the panel's honesty. But the murmur assumed a tinge of surprise verging on disapproval when Mrs. Han, plainly the youngest candidate, rose matter-of-factly and approached the rostrum. The two seated Nobels looked up with a start, while O'Kearn, still brandishing the envelope, stood watching her attentively. Not the least unnerved, Betty mounted the three steps and stopped in front of him. He handed her the envelope; she examined it carefully and returned it.

"Are you satisfied?" the chairman asked.

"Perfectly satisfied, sir."

"So you didn't quite trust us?"

"At a time like this, sir," she replied coolly, "I don't trust anyone, not even three Nobels."

O'Kearn stared at her fixedly, then nodded his head. Fawell, who knew him inside out, took this as a gesture of approval. She was right, he told himself. Chalk one up for her.

Betty had returned to her seat. In awesome silence O'Kearn opened the envelope and drew out the examination sheets: sixteen sets, each two pages long. He handed one to each of his colleagues, kept one for himself, and gave the rest to the usher for distribution. When all copies were given out, he cleared his throat and began speaking rather solemnly. "Madam and gentlemen, each of you is now in possession of the topics, or rather topic, for there is only one in this final examination. I ask you to listen closely and to stop me if there is something you don't understand."

After a pause during which the candidates bent over their papers, he began reading:

"CONTEST TO FILL THE OFFICE OF
PRESIDENT OF THE SCIENTIFIC
WORLD GOVERNMENT . . ."

He broke off to explain that a recapitulation of the contest's object and rules preceded the exam question proper; he then resumed reading:

"The candidates are reminded that this contest, the first of its kind, is open only to previously designated members of the world government. The latter have been selected to constitute this body on the basis of an examination testing the scope and quality of their knowledge of the principal matters affecting the future of the earth and mankind.

"The specific aim of this final examination therefore is to single out the most qualified individual among you to preside over the existing world government.

"The candidate judged by the full board of Nobel examiners to have turned in the best paper on the subject described hereunder will automatically assume the duties of chief executive.

"Also in accordance with the same panel's decision, not subject to appeal, the candidate handing in the second-best essay will be appointed vice-president and summoned to replace the chief executive in case of the latter's death or incapacitation.

"The other finalists will be assigned to various administrative offices at the president's discretion. Each will be ranked according to his standing in this examination, and those numbers will determine automatically the promotion of a new vice-president in case of the latter's death or incapacitation.

"The Scientific World Government, or SWG, will begin operating as soon as the results are announced, at which time the provisional administration now exercised by the Nobel assembly will cease. This SWG will function for nine full years unless directed otherwise by an absolute majority of the Nobels, in whose presence it must convene each time a significant decision is about to be made and, in any case, at least once a year for evaluation of its work."

Lowering his paper, O'Kearn paused to ask, "Is this clear?"

With unanimous consent, he continued, "Now we come to the examination topic."

"The candidates will outline their ideal program for the nine-year term of office, indicating the orientation, thrust, priorities, and so on, which each would give the program if he or she became president.

"Note especially: The subject is to be treated in a rigorously scientific way, but candidates may, at their own option, draw on nonscientific considerations such as popular needs and aspirations. No restriction or limitation shall bind them."

That was all. Once again O'Kearn asked if everyone had understood and if there were any questions. Then, glancing up at the clock, he said, "All right, madam and gentlemen, the examination is now beginning. It is May tenth, at ten minutes past nine. Your term of office, as you know, is nine years, so you have nine full days in which to do your essay. On May nineteenth at ten minutes past nine your papers will be collected. I remind you that no documents are to be consulted, and I trust that the topic will inspire you."

Before settling down to write, Fawell lingered for a while watching some of the other contestants already hunched over their desks. He exchanged a comradely wink first with Betty, then with Yranne, both of whom were also musing, probably trying to collect their thoughts before getting to work. A sense of intellectual kinship with his friends gradually dissolved the tension that had been paralyzing him since the start of the session. Now he felt relaxed and confident.

He gazed at the platform where the three Nobels were conversing in low voices. Behind them, perched on pedestals, was a series of busts of celebrated scientists, patron saints of the scientific era. At first only three busts had been given the place of honor in the huge amphitheater: Galileo, Newton, and Einstein. But this exclusive choice of physicists had evoked loud protest from the Nobel physiologists, resulting in the addition of several statues commemorating their own great masters. Still, the physicists had managed to place Einstein in the center, on a pedestal elevated ever so slightly above his neighbors.

In a less conspicuous corner of the hall there was also a smiling likeness of citizen Gary Davis. Though not in a class with the scientific geniuses, he had been a pioneer of world government and as such deserved to be remembered here.

Without really knowing why, Fawell smiled at all of them, then set to work confidently.

3

THE SCIENTISTS' revolution, or "Nobel conspiracy" as some called it (wrongly, for the initiative had not come from Nobels), had taken definite shape in California, among a handful of scientists in an atomic city sprung up around a giant betatron and several instruments of that kind, at once monstrous and delicate. Having come there to do research that was gradually penetrating the structure of matter, physicists from all over the globe enjoyed getting together with colleagues at the end of the day to compare notes, to discuss one theory or another, or simply to exchange ideas. Most of these gatherings were small groups of a truly international character. For several years now, Soviet and Asian scientists had been authorized, and had made it a practice, to spend periods of time in the atom city where they conversed as freely as the ranking scientists from the Western world.

But if the idea ripened there, and the will and plan to

achieve it, this was simply the final lap of a long scientific journey of the mind which had been under way for some time in all the countries. In the course of increasingly frequent meetings and discussions, the scientists had come to regard themselves as the one true international body, the only valid one, based on knowledge and understanding. Science, they felt, was both the soul of the universe and the single force capable of fulfilling human destiny once having wrested mankind from the trivial, infantile preoccupations of ignorant, verbose politicians. Gradually, out of many amicable, almost fraternal, discussions, emerged the vision of a glorious future, a planet united at last under the guidance of learning and wisdom. Thus far these were only blurred ideas and yearnings, but those sharing them — without giving any thought yet to their practical application — felt that they reflected factual reality and common sense.

The spark had sprung up almost simultaneously in the minds of a handful of relatively young scientists, who were guests of Fawell in the bungalow he and his daughter occupied. After an early marriage, he had lost his wife when Ruth was still a child; his work had absorbed him more and more, and he had never remarried. Ruth — who had little interest in intellectual pursuits but took them up all the same to please her father — kept house for him, which was not a chore in the light of his indifference to material things.

A trifling incident triggered the sudden burst of thought, a television program that managed to exasperate the normally unruffled dispositions of a few colleagues who had come by for a drink after a long day's work. Besides several physicists of various nationalities, there was Yranne the mathematician, who, in addition to his own research (which he could do anywhere as it required only a pencil and paper), was in the habit of putting his analytical talents to work for others. Betty Han had also come. Whenever in the area, she never lost a chance to see her friends.

After serving the drinks and checking to see that refills were at hand, Ruth excused herself, anticipating the usual shoptalk. But the shoptalk lagged after she left, and soon was dropped. Tonight, and quite independently, they all seemed obsessed by some idea that distracted them from their favorite topics. After glancing at his guests, Fawell turned on television. They listened, glasses in hand, and watched, a peculiar expression on their tense, frowning faces betraying general irritation. It was a trite interview with a prominent politician offering his opinions on domestic and foreign affairs, and went on for a quarter of an hour. Finally, when the comments became too painfully inane for him and everyone else, Fawell snapped off the set and faced his friends.

"You heard it and so did I," he told them. "The same thing day in and day out, or nearly the same, with a few variations. The same drivel constantly poured out by men who claim to be governing this country."

An Englishman, on a short course of training at the betatron, asserted that the same rubbish was daily fare in Britain.

"I've heard far worse in France," Yranne declared.

An Italian volunteered that political utterances in his country were every bit as childish as those they had just heard. From all corners of the room came the same protests: "Outrageous!" "Intolerable!"

All they had actually heard were the usual clichés from official or semiofficial sources. The average listener would not have been offended; ordinarily, the scientists themselves paid scant attention to such annoyances. Tonight, however, every trace of resignation had vanished.

"Intolerable is right," Fawell insisted in an odd voice that made everyone stare at him.

He paused, then went on, hammering out the syllables. "In-tol-er-a-ble. On that we all agree. Does anyone take issue if I say that what is intolerable ought not to be tolerated?"

"I'd be the last one," said Yranne the mathematician.

"Then it is our duty to act. . . ."

He was about to continue when a newcomer burst into the room. The sudden apparition in bedroom slippers and pajama top, hair and clothes awry, might have alarmed even this most informal circle of friends had it not been the astronomer Zarratoff, who was visiting the United States and presently spending a few days with Yranne, one of his best friends. He was known for his absentmindedness, his fits of enthusiasm, his passionate dedication to astronomy — a passion translating itself at times into lyrical outbursts — and for his superb chess, at which only Yranne, of all the amateurs, could beat him now and then.

"What's happened to you?" Fawell inquired mildly. "We didn't expect you this evening. Yranne told me you were working. Not that you aren't welcome, for you certainly are."

As a matter of fact, Yranne had left the astronomer in his room in a typical attitude, gazing intently at a map of the sky spread out before him, looking up only long enough to make brief notes interspersed with complex calculations. Knowing there was little chance of distracting Zarratoff when he was so absorbed, Yranne had simply told Fawell not to expect the astronomer that evening.

"Excuse me," Zarratoff apologized, looking distraught. "I couldn't take it any longer. I had to talk to someone. I rushed out of my room. . . . It was the television."

"Television?"

Gulping down the drink Fawell had just handed him, he went on to explain, "I was working, yes, but getting nowhere. I felt trapped in a web of contradictions. Then I got the absurd idea that watching television might relax my mind."

"Now I see," said Betty. "He must have heard the interview."

"Not that!" Zarratoff protested. "What do you think I am? I saw what I was in for there and switched channels after the first few words. I picked up channel three. Now do you follow me?"

"So what happened?"

"What happened? Well, if you weren't watching three, you obviously wouldn't understand."

"What was on three?"

"Games!"

"Games?"

"Yes, games," the astronomer moaned plaintively.

"I see," Yranne murmured.

"I know what you mean," added Fawell, sighing.

The scientists all shared the astronomer's distress and seemed truly sympathetic, without needing further explanations. He tried to make one anyway, still in the same pitiful voice as if invoking the heavens to witness his misfortune.

"Games, don't you see? What they call games! Even when rational creatures must be trying desperately to contact us on unknown wavelengths from somewhere in the Universe, those people split up into two teams of twelve and proceed to entertain themselves with a tug of war, cheered on by an ecstatic crowd. When there are —"

"Easy does it, old chap," Yranne interjected. "We all understand and share your indignation. Just tell us your conclusion. What did you think of it?"

"Intolerable!" shouted Zarratoff.

Everyone laughed.

"Then we all agree," Fawell said. "Relax and finish your drink. You came just in time."

They filled him in on the plan they were formulating and the discussion continued.

4

"As I WAS saying," Fawell went on, "today it is our imperative duty to end this situation. We have no right to let the world go to ruin. All scientists in this country will agree."

"In France too," Yranne declared. "I guarantee it."

"And in Britain," asserted the Englishman. "But what about the Soviet Union?"

Zarratoff hastened to reply: "Only thirty years ago one would have hesitated to answer that question. The fact of being held in suspicion by part of the world, you know, fostered a dangerous streak of nationalism which infected even our greatest scientists. Now that that distrust seems a thing of the past and we, like yourselves, have discovered just how incompetent our leaders are, I assure you that it no longer exists and that all men of science worthy of the name advocate a rational world organization. There is nothing surprising about this, I might add. Were we not the pioneers of internationalism?"

Everyone applauded his words. Without further discussion, they reached a common conclusion: In the current stage of evolution, a scientific world government was vitally necessary to mankind. Still, a few objections were raised as one would expect from persons trained to analyze objectively all the given facts of a problem.

"Scientists all over the world support this, true enough," said Yranne. "But that doesn't account for the masses, or the young people."

"I can vouch for Ruth," Fawell asserted, "and all her friends."

"Nicholas too," said Zarratoff. "We've often discussed it."

"Ruth and Nicholas may have been influenced by the intellectual milieu in which they were raised. . . . But can we really be so sure of all scientists? The Chinese, for instance?"

"Betty, there's a question for you."

"I think I can reassure you on that score," she replied, puckering up her eyes with their elongated pupils. "I am quite often in contact with my most eminent countrymen and have had occasion to sound some of them out — discreetly, of course — on the timeliness of such a revolution. Tonight's discussion is not new to me. All along I have felt that sooner or later you would be compelled to act. My inquiries led me to conclude that they all agree with you on the vital need for an international body; this in itself is no novelty, but they also share your conviction that you and they alone must comprise such a body and that the only central government capable of imposing its authority and worthy of governing the world is a scientific government. Believe me, they are fed up with infantile leadership. Stupidity, alas, is also international."

"Delighted to hear that. But what about the people? Let's have your opinion as a psychologist. Will they accept this revolution?"

Betty Han paused before answering, her eyes narrowing still further, a mark of intense concentration on her part.

"Possibly," she said at last. "It will be difficult. First I would like to find out what action you contemplate. Have you made a practical plan for taking power?"

They glanced at each other sheepishly. No hint of a plan, practical or otherwise, had seen the light, but that did not seem to trouble Fawell or his fellow physicists. They were aware that a sound idea ultimately finds its application, or, in their own terms, that experience sooner or later substantiates a valid theory. Besides, their basic principle was unassailable. The mathematician Yranne reiterated it, condensing it into a syllogism with self-evident premises: "That which is intolerable is not to be tolerated; allowing the Universe to crumble away into nations ruled by idiots is intolerable; therefore this condition must be ended."

"Let's not forget that there are practical problems," Betty reminded them.

"Aren't we used to overcoming problems?"

"What problems?" Zarratoff demanded vehemently. "We are dealing with ignorant people, and ours is the power born of knowledge. You physicists, didn't you invent insuperable weapons?"

"We created them, yes, but unfortunately," Fawell lamented, "we no longer control them. Our discoveries now belong to an army of industrialists, technicians, and workers. We need solid backing from all of them if we are to impose our authority and make it stick. Can we rely on their loyalty? Do we want it? Personally, I see it as a threat."

Others shared his fear, for the greatest foe of scientific inquiry was industrial technology. After a short discussion, everyone agreed that such an alliance would be risky and contrary to the ideal of their revolution — pure science.

"Even if we succeeded," Yranne concluded, "our enterprise would lead inevitably to a world take-over by a giant industrial mafia with crass interests and a mechanized system of government slanted toward increased production of consumer goods —"

"Which we certainly don't want," Fawell cut in sharply, "having glimpsed it in miniature already in this country."

"Or else toward a world dictatorship of the proletariat . . ."

"What a catastrophic prospect in this day and age!" the Russian Zarratoff declared.

"I feel the same way," said Betty Han.

Fawell pressed his conviction that, whereas technicians and industrialists would have a definite role to play, Science must maintain absolute control and direction of all projected action. Everyone agreed.

"This calls for the threat of a new invincible weapon, its secret known only to scientists," Zarratoff went on. "Doesn't such a thing exist? I'm only a theoretical astronomer and Yranne a mathematician, neither of us capable of practical achievements. But you physicists, don't you have a small deadly ray or two up your sleeve, the mere threat of which would bring all those imbeciles to their knees?"

"Impossible," Fawell retorted. "Not that such a thing couldn't be invented if we really put our minds to it, but there again, any practical application would involve the ranks of technology and industry. We're back with the same old problem."

"If, all by itself, your physics is incapable of performing concrete functions, then our plans are rather futile."

"Listen, Zarratoff," said Fawell. "I'll tell you a story that will give you some idea of our potential. It happened a few years ago when I was working for O'Kearn, the greatest living physicist, in his laboratory. He had already received the Nobel prize. I was his senior assistant, in charge of the lab, whose guiding spirit was O'Kearn. I had been there two years with a dozen research workers younger than I but highly competent. (The chief instructed me to weed out the incompetent ones ruthlessly, not to mention those he suspected of a lack of imagination.) All of them had excellent academic credentials and several years' experience in applied physics. A number of important discoveries came out of that laboratory."

"We know all that."

"Well then, besides some very delicate equipment, we had several ordinary electric motors, including a standard synchronous one — rather weak, only one or two kilowatts, as I recall — the type you find in the average shop. A mechanic took care of the machines.

"One evening I quit the lab and let two of my best researchers continue working for a few hours on an experiment they were eager to finish. I was home and just about to go to bed when one of them knocked on the door. He looked sheepish.

" 'What's the matter?' I asked. 'An accident?'

"I was worried, for the experiment involved releasing

substantial energy, and if poorly conducted could have blown the lab to bits and half the city with it. But I trusted my two assistants and was right to do so. Hastily, he reassured me.

" 'No, just a minor hitch which we ought to straighten out right away. I thought I should consult you.'

" 'A wise decision. Now what's the matter?'

" 'Well, it's the synchronous motor.'

" 'What about it? Did it break down?'

" 'Just the opposite.'

" 'What do you mean, the opposite?'

"He was growing more embarrassed by the minute. 'It's running,' he said, avoiding my eyes.

" 'So? Isn't it running properly? Speak up!' I prodded him.

"Blushing, he finally blurted out, 'It's running and I can't stop it. Joey left and forgot to do it. The control panel is Greek to me, and pressing one wrong button could cause a lot of damage.'

"Joey was our mechanic. I forget his last name, but I can still see him — a placid Negro, uneducated yet very conscientious about his job. It was the first time he had been careless.

"I whistled. 'What a nuisance! You really have a problem don't you? Imagine waking up the lab director to pull a lever and press a button! You're all alone there?'

" 'No, the other assistant is with me, but . . .'

" 'But what?'

" 'He's in the same boat; he doesn't know how to stop the motor either. We can't let it run all night.'

"I couldn't argue with that. Despite my annoyance, I would have to go with him. I slipped some clothes over my pajamas, and grumbling, I prepared to follow him.

"I had gone through those motions without even thinking, simply groaning at my responsibility. We headed for the lab, which, fortunately, was not far away. Something occurred to me and I stopped and said to him, 'By the way, don't you think it might have been simpler to wake up Joey?'

"Raising his eyes helplessly, he replied that they had spent two hours trying to locate Joey, who was nowhere to be found. This merely added to my irritation, for I must confess that, after working there two years, I realized only then that I had no idea how to stop the motor."

"I thought so," said Betty.

"But there was no retreating and we entered the lab. The motor appeared to be operating normally under the anxious scrutiny of the other assistant, who heaved a sigh of relief when I came in. It was a very painful experience, standing in front of that control board, not daring to touch any knob for fear of causing an accident. I hesitated, then decided to confess my ignorance to the two young men and give us all a laugh. 'We have to do something,' I said finally. 'There must be a circuit diagram somewhere.'

"We started rummaging through the cupboards and drawers. A waste of effort. Not a shred of information about the control panel, its shiny brass knobs assiduously polished every day by Joey. The motor went on whirring, taunting us with its sarcastic hum.

"There we were, all three of us trying to trace wires that vanished into vulcanite, when the door opened and in walked O'Kearn. Returning from a movie, the chief had seen a light in the lab and came to investigate. The shame of having to admit our incompetence was tempered by the relief of knowing that our troubles were over. I explained the situation to him at once.

"His reactions matched my own. First the sly gleam in his eye, then the irritation and the frown. At that point, I understood. He himself, the century's greatest scientist, the founder of this research center, was unable to stop this ordinary motor. We stared at each other. He has a sense of humor and both of us burst out laughing.

"The rest of the story doesn't matter. I set up a watch and had the two assistants take turns keeping an eye on the motor for the rest of the night — though I don't know why, for if it had suddenly gone out of kilter, no one could have done a thing about it. At least that way we were able to grease the bearings a little from time to time, as I remembered having seen Joey do. Everything worked out in the long run, and when Joey appeared the next morning, the machine came to an obliging halt the moment he touched a knob. I needn't tell you all the names we called him, poor fellow. And that's the story, Zarratoff."

"I get the point," said Yranne. "Too bad, because I had an interesting suggestion to make: Why don't you atomic scientists, rulers of energy, think up a way to alter the earth's axis of rotation and totally disrupt the climate? No one would defy the threat of such a disaster. I'm sure you'll say it would be child's play, providing you had an army of Joeys."

"Probably, but you know perfectly well that given our present level of knowledge, it couldn't be done."

"Indeed I know it," Yranne persisted, clinging fondly to his own idea. "All of us here know it, but not the blockheads who govern us. Spread it around that you have made such a discovery. Drum up a little publicity and then dangle your threat. They took the atomic bomb for a miracle. They're prepared to welcome another wonderwork of yours. They'll swallow this whopper like a peppermint drop and take fright. I mean it seriously."

"Right!" Zarratoff broke in. "Only once in my life did I talk to a government official. It didn't take me long to realize that he prided himself on knowing that the earth revolves around the sun. That was about all he knew. He had never learned that the sun is a star, and the Milky Way was only a poetic image to him, without real significance."

"What does our psychologist think?" Fawell asked.

"I think that with a little skill we could make them swallow just about any old nonsense, but I doubt that it would be politic. That kind of threat would discredit us in the eyes of the world, meaning the people, whose support we need — or at least their benevolent neutrality. We would be accused of trying to install a dictatorship. That's not the way we ought to proceed."

"How, then?"

Betty Han paused, her lovely eyes narrowing to slits. "Our strength lies in our intellectual prestige. We must preserve and reinforce it at all costs. The answer is a revolution that everyone accepts. Now don't jump on me! I think it would be very easy, far easier than your ultimatum backed by threats. All we need is to persuade every chief of state to transfer power to us."

"All we need! They'll never consent."

"Yes, they will," Betty declared, "and the people will support us if our plan is well presented and sponsored by reputable authorities. After the first shocks and grumbles wear off, I feel confident that they will yield and will even be grateful to us for relieving them of an intolerable burden, their responsibilities having expanded out of all proportion to their narrow minds."

"A definite shift seems to have taken place in recent

years among the political sects," Fawell observed. "A certain dread of power has emerged, combined with a still-dim awareness of their own mediocrity and the inept handling of current problems on the part of political leaders. I recall at least two instances somewhere in the world when there was serious difficulty electing a chief of state. The candidates hesitated to come forward, and those who finally did lacked enthusiasm."

"You see what I mean. If you give them a chance to fade away with dignity, they will grab it. And the public will cheer us. After a long, sad series of experiments, now recognized as the disasters they were, even the people are beginning to realize that their leaders have always been inept. Still, I repeat that we must act shrewdly and play all our trumps."

"What do you mean by that?"

"I see our success as dependent on at least two conditions. The first is that our enterprise be sponsored and introduced by the foremost scientific personalities. And when I say that" — Mrs. Han paused momentarily, lowered her voice, then went on — "I mean not just scientists but *celebrities,* people whose utterances go unquestioned because everyone up and down the social ladder regards them as symbols of wisdom and understanding. I don't want to offend you, Fawell, or you, Yranne. Both of you are just as qualified as the others I mention, if not more so, but you have no chance of gaining broad support if you present the plan for a world government as your own. Only the others can carry it off."

A long, meditative silence greeted her words.

"I understand," Zarratoff murmured at last.

"I do too," Fawell added. "You mean the Nobels."

"Exactly. We need them on our side, and maybe even to launch the project. Without them, we're helpless; with them, we can do anything."

"Yes, the Nobels are a condition of success," Fawell murmured pensively. "Psychology has its merits."

After further reflection, they all agreed. Betty Han continued, "Then our line of attack is drawn. Fawell, you are close to the most eminent and influential of them all. O'Kearn is the one you must contact first and win over."

The physicist stood up. "I'll take the night plane to New York and see O'Kearn in the morning," he declared. "But we don't want him to think this is a single individual's brainstorm. You must come with me."

After talking it over, they decided to send a delegation to the dean of Nobels: Fawell, Yranne, Mrs. Han, and Zarratoff. The four carried enough weight and represented sufficiently broad and varied scentific backgrounds to speak for everyone.

When that was settled, Fawell turned to Betty: "You mentioned two conditions essential to success, Betty. What do you see as the second one?"

"Enthusiasm. We will have to surround our plan with a tide of passion."

They stared at her curiously. Mrs. Han really had a unique way of describing enthusiasm and passion, displaying the utter composure of a mathematician demonstrating a geometric theorem. She went on: "The participation of the Nobels can prime a movement such as this, but I doubt that it will be enough."

"So?"

"So later on we'll find ways to stir up excitement. And there are ways."

As they were leaving to prepare for the trip, Fawell noticed Yranne's absent expression in contrast to the animated faces of his colleagues. "Something wrong?" he asked the mathematician. "Don't you think we ought to call in O'Kearn and the Nobels?"

Yranne shook his head. "Just a freakish idea, that's all, without rhyme or reason. Not worth repeating."

"Come on, what is it?"

Yranne burst out laughing. "After hearing your story, suddenly I began wondering if it wouldn't be better to call in Joey."

5

It was the fourth day of the final contest. Once again the thirteen candidates took their seats in the amphitheater where three Nobels proctored by turns. Fawell drew some smudged notes out of his briefcase and read them over rapidly — his work during the past three days. He had two reasons to be satisfied: the knowledge of having handled his subject well, and a feeling of relief that an essential but tedious phase was now behind him. Today at last he could address himself to the central issues.

This first part of his program dealt with overcoming as soon as possible the physical problems that impede human progress by subjecting mankind to ill health and a permanent state of anxiety. He gave priority to those matters not only because he believed that nothing significant could ever be achieved on earth as long as men were plagued by hunger, disease, and the bondage of labor, but also because secretly he intended to jolt his examiners.

Undoubtedly they would expect him, an expert in nuclear physics, to mobilize the globe for an accelerated and at last coherent program of atomic research. As a matter of fact, instinct and his faith in Science had suggested just that at first; but after thinking it over, he had decided that some kind of preliminary reorganization was needed, and to demand time for this would mark the lofty idealism desirable in a world leader.

Besides, he remembered a lively debate among Nobels at a meeting in which the structure of such a world government had been under discussion. The physicists were interested solely in scientific advances in their own field, namely, acquiring complete understanding of inorganic matter through analysis of infinitesimal particles. They were tartly reminded by physiologist and medical colleagues that the planet Earth was a non-negligible element of the universe, a fact they tended to overlook, and that its inhabitants were creatures possessing a quality called Life — specifically human beings with animal organisms subject to a variety of needs and damages, which Science ought not to ignore. Even if the cells of this organism ultimately could be broken down into atoms and electrons, that was no reason to neglect its structure or the study of its biology, in the aim of improving human development. Against his instincts, then, Fawell decided to deal first with man and his physical existence.

The best approach to the problem, he felt, was to determine the ideal global population, taking into account the planet's resources. He had discussed this point, quoting from various sources which his prodigious memory recalled, but still dissatisfied that lack of documentation ruled out a more accurate estimate. In any event, the figure he arrived at seemed a reasonable approximation, and he presented it as such: roughly four billion human beings. He gave a number of highly persuasive arguments to explain why it was essential not to exceed that figure.

At the same time he denied any intention on his part to promote an era of test-tube babies in the spirit of Aldous Huxley. One of his central concerns was to avoid indulging in such excess, an attitude shared by most scientists his age. Birth control undoubtedly would need to be strictly enforced at the start, but once its enormous benefits were understood, people would be likely to adopt it voluntarily.

Three years was the time limit for settling these basic problems. He listed them, then discussed two in detail, choosing what appeared to be the most pressing and the most haunting: world hunger and cancer.

He explained that the problem of hunger was relatively easy to solve, and that it still remained a problem only because of laziness, inexperience, and lack of cooperation among governments. A temporary solution could be reached in a month or so by commandeering all available military transport — and God knows there was enough of it around! Wartime fleets alone, with their gigantic vessels, their tens of thousands of planes and helicopters, when released by the stroke of a pen, would suffice amply (he proved this arithmetically) to transport vast quantities of surplus from overproducing countries to less fortunate regions afflicted with periodic famine. Combined with this, an in-depth study taking into account optimum population density would indicate the exact acreage to place under cultivation in any given area of the globe, as well as the type and quantity of fertilizers required, which could then be produced, and would allow rapid construction of irrigation systems on an undreamed-of scale. According to his scheme, a high proportion of current deserts could be made arable and the problem of hunger solved once and for all in three years at the utmost.

He allotted his administration the same period of time to eleminate cancer. There, too, without possessing special expertise, he had enough facts at hand to advance the following opinion supported by approximate figures: "Given the progress in research, even though this research is random and incoherent in all countries, performed for the most part under the shabbiest conditions and with inadequate funding; given the high caliber of research workers [a compliment calculated to woo Nobel physiologists away from their predictable reluctance to endorse a physicist as chief of state], there is every reason to anticipate that these efforts will achieve their goal very quickly once they are coordinated and adequately financed. All that is needed, I believe, is to establish an agency such as NASA — not for the same purpose, of course, but with the same purposeful dedication — the *unique aim* of which would be to rid mankind of cancer in three years, and to provide this agency with the means to achieve its task."

In dealing with facilities and funds for these enterprises, without going into great detail, which he felt was outside the scope of his subject, Fawell indicated that he bore them in mind constantly. In a few paragraphs he touched on the enormous resources which would be available to his government by virtue of its being global, and the spectacular savings that would result, in contrast to previous wasteful administrations. One such saving, though not the most important, fairly leaped off the page, yet he decided to mention it first and with a tinge of humor, something that a few Nobels occasionally appreciated: He called for immediate abolition of foreign ministries all over the world.

The other benefits were far more significant and just as manifest: doing away with war departments; dismantling armies and armaments, except those needed by the government to maintain order; reducing the remaining government bureaus to a handful of central agencies, a far less costly arrangement than time-honored dispersion.

Many other problems needed solving if the planet was to be properly reorganized. To save time, Fawell contented himself with simply mentioning them and outlining possible answers. In broad terms then, he had covered trade, currency, language, and labor regulations, proposing that an effective agency be created to handle each sensitive issue. Once again he used NASA to illustrate that just about anything could be accomplished by using bold and rational methods. If some of NASA's achievements were not as important or as urgent as many others from a strictly scientific point of view, the responsibility resided with the politicians who called for them. (Fawell knew that most Nobels had opposed the Apollo program in its day.) In the future, it would be up to a government of scientists to set goals in terms of reasonable priorities, and it seemed evident that such agencies could carry out successfully the most demanding tasks.

6

HAVING DEALT with the problems of physical existence and outlined the measures needed to bring order to a planet long since abandoned to anarchy and neglect, Fawell now approached the domain of the mind, that noble and precious essence, the development of which was both the justification for and the distant ideal of a scientific world administration. Here at last was a topic that absorbed him completely, stirring every fiber of his being, demanding faith and passion as well as intellect.

For at the start of this twenty-first century, the mind was indeed of major concern to Fawell, as it was to Yranne, Zarratoff, and most revolutionary scientists, who, moreover, considered themselves materialists. For them, Science was a philosophy, verging on a religion: a religion whose enigmatic and presently inaccessible God was the essence of the Universe; whose sole acknowledged rite was unceasing research; whose creed, the knowledge of this universe, was singular in that each day it was re-explored, rejected, recovered, revived, and recreated by dint of strenuous, occasionally brilliant, speculation and by endlessly repeated experiments.

The nineteenth century's rigorous positivism was remote. In one short phrase Einstein had set its limits: "A theory can be verified by experiment, but there is no direct path from experiment to the creation of a theory." Later, he had often spoken of "cosmic religiosity," an expression that continued to fascinate astronomers like Zarratoff. In the years following, beginning with the second half of the twentieth century, metaphysics, discredited since Descartes's day, had started to reinvade Science; or at least physics because, curiously enough, most biologists rejected the trend in the name of intellectual austerity and went on maintaining that nothing exists outside our experience. But physicists like Fawell and devotees of cosmogony like Zarratoff were saturated with it. Perhaps this was due to the fact that their respective fields — one infinitely small, the other infinitely large — were known to defy direct observation the deeper one probed, forcing the intellect to speculate in order to compensate for instrumental shortcomings and, on occasion, to fill the void with mysteries.

If, during the twentieth century, a brief tide of deviationism had appeared momentarily to orient Science toward a dehumanized and aimless industrialization operated by robots and computers, the genuine scientists were not to blame for those heresies, and a reaction soon set in. First, a handful of thinkers defined the true aim of Science thus: the acquisition of knowledge and the gradual penetration of nature's secrets. Now, in this dawn of the twenty-first century, informed people accepted the definition for a fact, regarding this knowledge as mankind's sole objective. Rarely did they find any intrinsic interest in material or technological advances. They had pledged to relegate computers and other machines to the permanent rank of tools, useful and ingenious devices but nothing more. If Fawell found it acceptable, even indispensable, to develop practical applications of science, it was in the hope of freeing men from harsh, brutalizing toil and enabling them to devote an increasing part of their leisure to the one authentic progress he acknowledged: the acquisition of sacred knowledge.

So ran the thinking of scientists in this century. Their obsession was such that they planned to mobilize all the planet's resources in the service of their ideal, those inestimable riches hitherto squandered, diverted from their natural functions by petty questions of nationalism or ownership, or by antiquated beliefs rooted in superstition, in the dreams of false prophets and, generally, in the negation of reality.

There were, of course, slight variations in the image of this new deity embraced by the physicists. For some, it was entirely a product of the human mind; for others, a discovery and a conquest. The former spoke of "emergence"; although Bergson's remote influence was apparent, they were more likely to illustrate their beliefs with certain phrases of Professor Samuel Alexander. The world tends toward the Divinity, they would say, adding, as he did: it is not God who created the world but the world which is in the process of creating God, having done with human mediation.

Others, of a pantheistic cast, had undergone various influences, from Thales and his "all things are full of gods" to Teilhard de Chardin, with detours into J. B. S.

Haldane's dialectical materialism and a number of philosophic poets, some of whose salient precepts Zarratoff loved to quote: for example, "the drop of mind in matter."* But physicists in this group took Teilhard as their ultimate authority, interpreting his central philosophy thus: Inert matter does not exist. Evolution obeys a cosmic design; begun at the atomic level by the force of this cosmic consciousness diffused into every infinitesimal particle, carried on at the human level with an infinitely greater concentration of means, it should end in a total identification with the Universe through complete understanding of its mysteries.

There were, to be sure, a good many discrepancies between such simple assertions and the Christian principles of this Jesuit priest, which might have prompted him to repudiate the scientists as disciples, but they discounted such discrepancies as unimportant. Fawell was one of them, and in rejecting virtually the entire Christian content of Teilhard's creed, he continued to admire him as much as ever. His own God — the one he pursued in his passionate exploration of matter — he called "essence of the Universe," but whether one called it the universal Christ, or whether evolution was renamed "christogenesis" and the limit of total knowledge marking fusion "the Omega Point" remained for him purely a question of semantics, and so irrelevant. Friends with whom he discussed this did not always agree. Yranne and Zarratoff, for instance, came down harshly on Teilhard's attempted synthesis of Science and Christianity, and even labeled it casuistry.

Oddly enough, whenever such discussions got under way, Betty Han, who always kept one foot on the ground and probably was the least attracted to cosmic religiosity,

* Henri Fauconnier, *Malaisie* (trans. 1967 as *Soul of Malaya*)

invariably would fly to the defense of both scientist and priest. She did this in a curious, faintly ambiguous way, declaring that in her opinion as a professional psychologist, this synthesis represented the most eloquent example she knew of the human mind's desperate attempts to impose an artificial harmony on incongruous, if not plainly contradictory, elements. She declared her unqualified admiration for this impassioned, nearly successful effort, expressing the view that if casuistry really was involved, then it was inspired casuistry, to which she surrendered enthusiastically. This last remark drew silent, quizzical stares from everyone, for the image of an "enthusiastic" Betty struck her friends as puzzling, if not preposterous.

Whether the physicists envisaged the total creation of a god, or the discovery and assimilation of one, they were more or less agreed on an ideal situated in the future and on the sanctity of knowledge. The biologists also gave priority to knowledge (one of the few philosophic concepts the two groups shared) but fiercely resisted the lure of metaphysics.

That had not always been the case. During the first half of the twentieth century, a number of them had used the mathematics of probability and examples focused on monkey typists to attempt to demonstrate that the emergence of the human brain was a phenomenon so improbable as to constitute an impossibility, without evolution having taken a supranatural direction. But contemporary biologists as well as physicists now rejected this theory, the former arguing that if the combinations of atoms which developed into the brain and consciousness were quasi-impossible, then all other combinations must have displayed the same quasi-impossibility. Just as in a lottery involving billions of billions of billions of tickets, one of those tickets has to turn up, bearing a certain number, the drawing of that particular number assuming *a priori* a character as miraculous as the organization of the human brain. On intellectual grounds therefore, they had no reason not to accept the latter as an effect of probability, and they did, a probability so extraordinary that there was no chance of it ever recurring in the universe.

The physicists, confirmed materialists in the then-accepted sense of the word, were equally opposed to the notion of a *supranatural* power controlling evolution. Fawell blamed the reasoning of earlier mathematical biologists for treating atoms like marbles and physical bodies like sacks of marbles. To the latter one might properly apply the theory of probability, citing examples of monkeys at the typewriter; but all his theorizing and experimenting on infinitesimal particles had gradually convinced him that physical bodies bore no resemblance at all to sacks of inert marbles. Matter, he decided, was something quite different. . . . "Sacred Matter," he used to call it — another expression of Teilhard's, whom he could quote at length from memory — matter which, by its very nature, had given birth to thought, probably on many other planets besides Earth.

In short, biological and physical scientists had a fair number of differences. This rarely produced conflict as they had very little to do with each other, but conveyed itself in sarcastic, remotely launched sallies in which, paradoxically, the same word associated with a different meaning was used by both parties to castigate the opposition's philosophic inconsistencies. For instance, "anthropocentrists" expressed O'Kearn's contempt for the Nobel physiologists, implying that they considered man a unique miracle of probability and reduced the entire body of science to human observations. "Anthropocentrists" was also the epithet biologists cast at neo-materialist physicists to denote their absurd efforts to establish a qualitative relationship between the human brain and the cosmos. But in spite of this, the word was unlikely to crop up even in the stormy debates that occasionally brought them together, for both parties held it to be a supremely crude and defamatory insult calling for an apology.

This left the ideal of *knowledge* the common denominator for all scientific minds during this period. To physicists, it resembled a religion; to biologists, an ethic, a free act, the impelling necessity for which they vaguely discerned as an antidote to the despair of nothingness. Both agreed that this total understanding could be attained only through the collective efforts of all mankind. The world to which they aspired was in fact very unlike Huxley's "Best of Worlds."

Fawell took time to reflect before launching the second phase of his plan, organizing thoughts which had obsessed him during the night. His conclusion, bitterly disappointing, was dictated nevertheless by logic and by a realistic appraisal of world conditions. Certainly he felt a nagging urge to get started immediately on a systematic program of research, especially in his own still-mysterious field of infinitesimal matter, and to put all mankind straight to work on it, but the glaring fact remained that mankind was presently unequal to the task. It would take preparation, and the first government's nine-year term would allow barely enough time. Physical reorganization needed to be followed up by a long period of spiritual, namely educational, development.

Imagining himself in the highest post required no special effort on Fawell's part; the contest seemed to call for it. He sighed to think that *his* administration would be merely a transitional one, his function, his duty being to clear the way for the final leap. But it was unavoidable. This stage was bound to occupy at least four or five years, which, added to the previous three, left only one or two for dealing with the principal task. In this contest, which for him had come to represent reality on a small scale, he resolved to spend only one day outlining a program of basic research. Education would take up most of his remaining time.

He set to work on this next chapter, the education of a world freed at last from poverty and capable of lifting itself out of ignorance, provided the central administration had done its work of guidance in that direction. Here again Teilhard helped to illustrate his ideas. As epigraph, he quoted nearly word for word (capitals and all) a passage from *The Phenomenon of Man* that had come back to him the night before on the edge of sleep:

> . . . The moment will come — it is bound to — when Man will admit that Science is not an accessory occupation for him but an essential activity, a natural derivative of the overspill of energy constantly liberated by the Machine.
>
> We can envisage a world whose ever-increasing leisures and heightened interest will find their vital issue in exploring everything, trying everything, extending everything . . . a world in which, not only for special units of paid research workers, but also for the ordinary citizen, the day's goal would be the wresting of another secret or another force from corpuscles, stars, or organized matter.

Fawell spent most of the remaining time trying to hasten humanity's approach to that great moment. If he could bring it to the point of "sublimation of interest," as Wells* put it, he could do anything. To cross that threshold in a few years would not be easy. Wells had

* H. G. Wells, *The Shape of Things to Come*

predicted that it would take 150 years, but his modern state was not truly scientific. He did not aim high enough at the start. There was no reason not to progress much more rapidly.

After the epigraph, Fawell paused again to speculate, trying to imagine what the world would be like at the end of his nine-year term. Just then he thought of his daughter. It was the first time he had thought of her since the examination began, so absorbed had he been in the future. Ruth would probably experience the total glorious metamorphosis. She would not be even thirty at the end of his term.

It was thrilling to think what women like her and men like Nicholas Zarratoff would be able to do. But only if the task he had set himself succeeded. It would. Fawell swore that it would and went back to work.

7

O'KEARN'S GENIUS shaped the plan for a world government into final form and established the procedure for selecting its members. He greeted the delegation of young scientists cordially, as was his custom unless confronted with a scientific heresy, in which case he was apt to be ferocious. The introduction was brief since he already knew Fawell's three companions. Assuming that a visit so early in the morning involved something important, he urged his former assistant to come straight to the point. When Fawell had done so in a few sentences, the great scientist seemed neither surprised nor indignant.

"I often thought this would happen," he said. "My own belief all along has been that a world government would be necessary in the not-too-distant future. Einstein said so, and so do all our greatest experts too. Yet somehow I imagined it springing from the ashes of war, mankind's one last chance for survival, as Wells predicted.

You want to make a peaceful revolution. That's fine by me. In any case it's perfectly clear that such a government would have to be run by experts, I mean trained scientists. But have you stopped to think what a howl will go up when you suggest abolishing nations?"

"Science has already abolished them."

"That's true, but public opinion is not scientific. Don't forget, it isn't the first time this sort of plan has been proposed. Anyone who has ever mentioned a world administration or a world federation was brushed off as a dream merchant, a wishful thinker, a utopian. Even timid efforts at concentration and local cooperation, on the modest scale tried in Europe, aroused a storm of abuse and sarcasm. What will happen when you talk of world government? . . . Now I have the impression you don't agree, Mrs. Han. Tell me honestly what you think."

Unable to suppress a gesture of protest, Betty replied, "I simply would like to point out that all the abuse was delivered in the name of 'realism.' 'Unrealistic' is the usual label for anyone who invokes the natural law of concentration and proposes to accelerate its effects. 'Unrealistic' was the term of derision reserved for advocates of a European federation. Now I ask you, sir, how can that argument be used when we assert that government ought to be administered by the greatest realists of our time, the scientists?"

"Some people will use it anyway, but your point is a good one."

"I think Betty is right, sir," said Yranne. "You can get away with labeling theorists like myself starry-eyed dreamers, but not physicists who devote their lives to exploring and analyzing matter, to probing the deepest secrets of reality."

"Or those who spend every day examining the cells of life," Betty added.

O'Kearn's face clouded over. "Do I understand that you also want to enlist experts in the so-called natural sciences," he inquired with evident disdain. "Biologists? Physiologists?"

"After thinking about it, we decided it was essential."

The physics laureate apparently did not share their view. "Like Pythagoras and like Einstein, I believe that truth is independent of man," he declared. "Tell me, isn't truth the aim of Science?"

"I should think so," murmured Zarratoff.

"I agree, sir," Fawell pleaded, "but the conquest of truth is called knowledge or understanding. Well, in the present stage of evolution and in the world we know, this understanding requires the human brain."

"Without Einstein or someone of his caliber, the truth behind his theories would remain hidden," Betty insisted.

"It would still exist," O'Kearn muttered.

After thinking it over, however, the scientist grudgingly conceded they might be right and that any type of government ought to be concerned with people. Besides, the presence of biologists and doctors would make realism unassailable.

"Actually, I think you have a sensible plan, and I'll do whatever I can to help you," he told them. "But I'm getting old; I'm no man of action, and it will take a lot of energy and determination to govern the world. I don't think I could do it."

Fawell then explained why they felt it was essential to win support from the Nobels. Their solid backing alone could insure the plan's success.

"Whose idea was that?" the physicist asked.

All eyes rested on the Chinese psychologist.

He nodded. "It doesn't surprise me. It's an intelligent idea."

The approving nod gave way to a frown. "There are not only scientists among us. Even if you insist on including physiologists in that category, this still leaves the literary Nobels. Do you intend to recruit novelists and poets as well?"

The four envoys looked at each other in silent embarrassment.

Fawell finally spoke: "I have to admit that we never got to that question. What do you think, Betty?"

She replied instantly: "We need the sponsorship of every Nobel without exception. We need the literary Nobels to rally the aesthetes; we also need the peace laureates who have something vital to contribute. Yes, the peace element would be a great asset."

"I don't see how we can include writers in a scientific government," Fawell murmured. "A writer writes under the influence of contemporary taste. He is no innovator in the spiritual domain. But our government, which aims at discovering the unknown, must ignore taste. Wells put it this way: 'Aesthetic life is conditioned by the times, science conditions the times.' "*

"It's out of the question!" O'Kearn shouted, banging the table.

The visitors had won the first round: O'Kearn was now so committed to the project that he considered it his very own. In the last few minutes his whirring mind had begun framing a workable plan.

"No Nobel should be part of this government," he announced decisively. "It can only increase their prestige. Besides, most of them, like myself, are too old to be very active."

* H. G. Wells, *The Shape of Things to Come*

"But if they support us, they'll want to share the action."

"We must never permit it. Can't you just see that old jackass Alex Keene running the world? Why, he'd make a worse mess of it than we have now."

Sir Alex Keene was the ranking Nobel biologist, a bacteriology expert famous for his studies of microorganisms. Keene was O'Kearn's great rival and only a shade less prestigious.

"They won't ask for a thing if we provide them with purely honorary posts just to satisfy their egos. Pardon the expression, but I know my colleagues in 'Nobelry.' "

O'Kearn went on to describe the plan he had just formulated, the main features of which ultimately were put into operation. The Nobels first would lend moral support to the enterprise, then select members of the government based on the results of a competitive examination which they alone would judge. "And I give you my word," the scientist repeated, a glint of malice in his eyes, "not one of them will have the slightest desire to take the exam."

"Why?"

"Because virtually the whole lot of them will have been eliminated. Can you imagine Alex Keene struggling with problems of nuclear physics when he doesn't even know what an atom is? . . . And don't forget how extremely difficult the exam will be, requiring the broadest scientific learning. Only young men and women like yourselves will have the courage and endurance to undertake the intense preparation for it. . . . So, my children," he continued in a warmer vein, rubbing his hands, "you want to run the world? You'll have to prove worthy of it. I know already the kind of questions I shall ask you."

Happy to see their project under way, the four ambassadors took leave of O'Kearn after he had promised to get off immediately to all living Nobels a confidential letter stressing the vital decisions expected of them and urging them to attend a conference.

"I can see them now," said O'Kearn, who was inclined to exercise his caustic wit at his colleagues' expense. "They'll turn up itching with curiosity, puffed up with pride. The rest you can leave to me. I'll handle it."

As he guided them out, O'Kearn whispered in Betty's ear, "Mrs. Han, I think you were absolutely right. We need all the Nobels, especially the peace laureates. Do you know why?"

"To inspire confidence in people all over the world, who yearn for peace."

"Yes, and also to keep peace among my colleagues. Did you think of that?"

"It wasn't precisely my main thesis, sir," Betty replied, her almond eyes narrowing, "but psychology apparently took it into account."

8

"TO ALL CHIEFS OF STATE:

Gentlemen . . ."

Thus began the letter addressed to leaders of all nations which the Nobels sent out at the close of a conference organized by O'Kearn, during which the plan for a world government received Nobel endorsement.

The conference was a success. After swearing his colleagues to secrecy, the renowned physicist described the plan, explaining that their support would entail placing their prestige, influence, and expertise behind it. His persuasive arguments easily obtained their unanimous endorsement. None of them had any use for the myopic policies of existing governments, which allotted beggarly grants to research projects not directly related to national defense. None of them could stand watching the earth's precious resources squandered dangerously, frivolously, or just senselessly while scientific endeavors had to go begging.

Excited applause greeted O'Kearn's speech. For once, the Nobels were of a single mind and eager to act. It was now simply a question of deciding how the scientists should go about seizing power. They began discussing it in small groups and in general sessions; this went on for two weeks. Then a letter was drafted, sent out to heads of state everywhere, published that same day in the world press and broadcast in the media, creating a great stir in all lands and all hearts. The letter read:

Gentlemen:

Before explaining the purpose of this message, we wish to remind you of the following facts, which are common knowledge and indisputable to anyone with opinions based on objective judgment.

The world we live in, the spiritual and physical world, has been shaped by Science, without which it would be merely the jungle preserve of animals. Science has contributed two essential elements, radiant poles for all rational beings:

1) Knowledge

2) Power

1 KNOWLEDGE: Everything man knows about the Universe in which he exists was discovered and taught by us, the men of science, a breed whose luminaries include Leucippus, Pythagoras, Galileo, Newton, Darwin, Pavlov, Einstein, and others still among us whose modesty we shall respect. Thanks to them (and, we venture to add, to us, their heirs and disciples who at least can understand and interpret their genius), the world now knows:

— That matter is composed of atoms.

— That these atoms are in turn made up of particles with

strange patterns of behavior, which we are now beginning to comprehend.

— That the human body, ours and yours, gentlemen, is composed of cells.

— That blood circulates throughout this body controlled by a muscle that acts like a pump. That the human heart can repair itself and can even be replaced when worn out.

— That atoms sometimes combine to form molecules. That these molecules in turn, through a process we are just beginning to understand, have massed together to form cells of organic matter.

— That the earth revolves. That it is not the center of the Universe but a mere speck of dust, similar to billions of other planets, satellites of billions of sister stars of our sun. That these stars are grouped in galaxies; that there are also billions of galaxies, themselves related to systems of galaxies, all of which form a space-time universe. That some of us are starting to measure this universe (which others maintain is immeasurable), to study its birth (which some deny), its aging, and to predict its death (which others reject). . . .

Each clause of this section had aroused bitter arguments inasmuch as not all the scientists endorsed particular assertions. When Betty finally got to read the letter (drafted entirely by the Nobels and kept secret until its publication), she wagered Fawell a dinner that the parenthetical remarks had been appended. The psychologist won the bet. As O'Kearn later confirmed, they were inserted to satisfy a minority fiercely opposed to accepted theories of the nature of the Universe.

The letter continued:

— That man is the product of a long evolution through various forms of animal life, the chain of which we have nearly succeeded in reconstructing.

— That the Universe does not obey Euclidean geometry.

— That the laws of statistics have a dominant effect on the organization of the physical universe. . . .

In this document composed by the world's leading scientists, each clause of which had been weighed and analyzed, it was rather odd that no logical order seemed to have been observed. The lengthy list gave the impression that ideas had been set down more or less at random as people thought of them.

Not so. The apparent disorder was the result of careful wording and of a last-ditch attempt on the part of Nobel peace laureates to placate the various experts who kept insisting that advances made in their own special scientific sectors receive top billing on the list.

In fact, the conference had been one protracted demonstration of rivalries between the two main clans of Nobel scientists, the physicists on the one hand, and the physiological and medical scientists on the other, with chemists joining the camp of their choice. The physicists — apart from metaphysical differences of opinion which O'Kearn, their acknowledged spokesman, had pointed out correctly — were interested in the Universe divorced from man or even life; whereas the others regarded the miracle of life on earth as the only authentic science. Their advocate, the celebrated bacteriologist Sir Alex Keene, would sniff contemptuously whenever O'Kearn's work was mentioned.

Considering themselves the only valid scientific authorities, the physicists had set to work drafting the first few clauses of the letter, mentioning scientific achievements exclusively in the domain of inorganic matter. Right at the start, a dispute broke out in their own ranks. A nuclear specialist urged precedence for the microscopic realm of the atom; another expert, responsive only to the laws of gigantic aggregations and author of an original theory of cosmology, insisted on priority for his macroscopic view of the world. The debate sharpened. Words — nucleon, meson, neutrino, antiparticle, from one side; nebulas, spirals, galaxies, quasars from the other — flew back and forth like bullets, until Sir Alex Keene, roused to such a pitch of indignation by this farrago, bellowed, "And where does that leave physiology, gentlemen?" without even suspecting that he had parodied a famous retort.*

His outburst cast a chill over the meeting until one of the literary Nobels, recalling a similar phrase from his childhood readings, checked its source, discovered the analogy, and passed it on to his colleagues. The scientists regained their good humor temporarily, but now the biologists felt their steam up and demanded preference on the list of mankind's major scientific achievements.

Voices rose. The discussion degenerated into a violent quarrel during which some people claimed they heard O'Kearn fling the supreme insult "anthropocentrist" at Sir Alex Keene. The latter paled with rage, and who knows what might have happened if the peace Nobels had not intervened promptly? At their urging, the physicist was willing to swear that he had never uttered the word, and, thanks to them, everyone gradually calmed down. Shuttling back and forth between the two clans, and racking their brains for solutions acceptable to both, the peace Nobels finally got them to agree to a delicately worded variant of the paragraph on scientific attainments. Some dreadful muddles developed from time to time;

* "Et que sera donc la philosophie?" from Molière's *Le Bourgeois Gentilhomme.*

Fawell deplored them while O'Kearn, unfailingly cordial to his colleagues, used them to display his biting wit.

The rest was easier and won instant approval from everyone.

. . . That, gentlemen, is a brief summary of the record achieved by knowledge. That is what the world knows, thanks to us. The next remark is important, therefore we have underlined it: *In this intellectual labor that has been progressing for a thousand years, in this uninterrupted chain of speculations, experiments, and systematic reasoning illumined by occasional flashes of genius, which in our view constitute mankind's essential task, none of you gentlemen has ever participated* [except perhaps Thomas Jefferson].

Like the host of officials performing functions you choose to call governmental, you have never experienced the drive to possess truth, and have remained generally more ignorant of the aforementioned achievements than the man in the street, who at least reads now and then.

We might add that not merely have you ignored our inspired efforts, but you have often opposed them. We have watched you stem this happily irresistible tide with all your might, withholding funds from research laboratories, which you then squandered aimlessly or in dangerous and criminal enterprises.

Because of your negligent or malevolent attitude, gentlemen, Science has not reached the peaks it should and could have reached, leaving a number of glaring gaps in our knowledge which redound to our humiliation and your disgrace.

At this very moment we do not know:

— The secret governing the primary mechanisms of the central nervous system.

— Whether the Universe will go on expanding perpetually

or ultimately contract.

— How to cure the common cold.

— What, precisely, is the structure of the atom. . . .

A list followed, the same length as the previous one and displaying the same lack of logical order for the same reasons. The first section of the letter concluded thus:

These and many other zones of darkness are far from inaccessible to penetration, but if they are to be explored, it will demand mobilization of all the physical and spiritual resources of our world, which you are squandering, and a rational global organization of scientific research, which you cannot even conceive, in peace and freedom, which are enigmas to your minds.

This, gentlemen, is the message we have sought to bring you about knowledge. We have been brief, knowing how unfamiliar you are with these matters, the scope of which escapes you. We will give more emphasis to the second treasure for which the world is indebted to us.

2 POWER: Besides the earliest inventions such as fire, which could only have been made by scientific thinkers, across the centuries we have given you:

— Dynamite

— Hygiene and vaccination (power over death)

— Electricity

— Antibiotics

— Atomic energy, nuclear energy, etc.

After another long list, the letter concluded its preamble thus:

In regard to this gradual wresting of power from nature, here again, gentlemen, you have not participated at all, but in this case your position is far worse: not only have you accepted these riches without understanding their meaning or even attempting to understand it, but you have deformed them to make them serve only your craving for comfort, your apathy and, by extension, the most odious of crimes, namely, the systematic murder of those you wildly label "foreigners."

Thus each time a discovery of ours has fallen into your inept or vicious hands (we apologize for the words, but we Nobels have weighed them carefully), you manage to corrupt its significance, to stifle the scientific spirit in which it was conceived, and ultimately to substitute a demon, the perversity Milton described thus:

> Fall'n Cherub, to be weak is miserable
> Doing or Suffering: but of this be sure,
> To do aught good never will be our task,
> But ever to do ill our sole delight,
> As being the contrary to his high will
> Whom we resist. If then his Providence
> Out of our evil seek to bring forth good,
> Our labour must be to pervert that end,
> And out of good still to find means of evil;
> Which oft-times may succeed. . . .*

This plainly was a contribution from the literary Nobels. At first the others had frowned and objected to having poetry appear in such a document, but the former stood their ground, and for having taken such a modest, almost humiliating, part in the proceedings thus far, were allowed finally to have their way. Until then in fact, despite manifest good will and a desire to cooperate, the literary laureates had confined their remarks to scattered pleas — peevishly spurned for the most part — for observance of the aesthetic creed they had forged in a lifetime of study. This creed relied entirely on eliminating

* *Paradise Lost*

most epithetical adjectives, inserting one or two elegant preterits where readers would anticipate an ordinary past tense and, most significantly, replacing all adverbs ending in "ly," such as "harmoniously" or "exclusively," by more satisfying expressions such as "in a harmonious manner," or "in an exclusive way." The more daring innovators among them were rash enough to propose substituting "at a snail's pace" for that atrocious word "slowly," but the majority of their colleagues would not venture that far.

The literary Nobels were furious that their proposals were not always carried, and it would have been cruel to deny them such innocent satisfaction. Besides, after hearing an explanation of Milton's verses and reflecting on it, the scientists granted that the quotation was highly appropriate in that Science thus could be interpreted as the symbol of Good, and political forces, of Evil. Any number of examples served to illustrate this:

We brought you fire. It was meant to warm you in winter and to cook your food. You used it to forge swords and to set cities ablaze.

We invented machines to ease man's lot. You transformed them into engines of death on land, on sea, and in the skies.

We gave you energy in all its forms. You have used it to wipe out whole regions. . . .

To conclude this preamble, gentlemen, we have evidence that you are totally unqualified to run this world or any part of it. The dreary facts of your tenure tell that you will all exhaust yourselves in puerile rivalries, in sterile discussions and petty wrangles before consuming whole nations in murderous wars contrary to the spirit of Science, wars you admit that you cannot avert, having done your utmost to ignite them through your own blindness, ignorance, and neglect.

We now come to the object of this message. We Nobels, gathered in plenary session — scientific Nobels, peace Nobels, literary Nobels — are of the unanimous opinion that it is your duty to end an abnormal and highly inflammatory situation.

We ask you therefore to perform the sole act by which you may be of some service to humanity: resign, divest yourselves of power and transfer it to Science, which will take charge of running the world in the best interests of its citizens. It is our opinion that Science alone can do this. Fumbling experiments by other international bodies have failed in the past, and were bound to fail because delegates accredited to insane governments were themselves inevitably devoid of intelligence and logic.

Gentlemen, we Nobels do not seek power for ourselves but to vest in people young enough to display dynamic leadership, people who have given evidence of wisdom and broad scientific understanding which we alone are qualified to judge.

After you have resigned — hopefully on receipt of this letter — and pending formation of the kind of government mankind desperately needs, we shall exercise provisional control over existing administrative agencies, which shall remain intact. Our elected officials will be responsible for concentrating the present amalgam into a few central, coherent administrative bureaus.

We have several additional observations to make. Despite our conviction that these facts cannot have failed to stir your conscience and impel you to step down, we have seen fit, in any event, to take the following precautions:

1) Irrespective of nationality, we have all exchanged the latest findings in our various fields of research. We stress that some of these findings would be of significant interest to you in connection with improving your own offense-

defense weaponry. We have also pledged that a discovery made by any one of us will be communicated instantly to all others.

2) Bear in mind — for surely this will have an immediate impact on you — that large numbers of obscure scientists recruited for your so-called national defense and hosts of technicians working on classified projects have been released from their oath of secrecy by us, the Nobels, and have agreed to follow our example.

Gentlemen, this is how things stand at the present moment:

— Soviet scientists and technicians are cognizant not only of the latest scientific theories developed in the United States relating to antimatter and cosmic radiation, but also of the industrial processes underlying the manufacture of our top-secret nuclear weapons, the precise range and accuracy of the latest American missiles as well as the number, strength, and exact location to within a yard of their stockpiles.

— In return, American scientists and technicians now know all there is to know about the Soviet armed forces, including the location of underground shelters for top military and government personnel.

— Similarly (these are random examples of the results of various efforts we have initiated), Chinese cryptanalysts can read the secret codes developed by fellow-mathematicians in other countries. Furthermore, Israeli code experts are now able to decipher top secret Chinese messages in a matter of minutes.

— As the final example of steps we Nobels have taken to secure a triumphant scientific revolution and the survival of mankind, we draw your attention to the fact that all research in the area of chemical and bacteriological warfare is now available to laboratories throughout the world.

We are enclosing copies of documents classified by you as top secret (industrial operations, location of various stockpiles, secret codes, et cetera) to demonstrate that our assertions are not idle boasts.

We trust, gentlemen, that Reason and our own reasoning will convince you of your unworthiness and of the necessity for your taking the step we have indicated without delay.

A list of signatures followed, in alphabetical order, of all living Nobels.

9

An INTERNATIONAL holiday was set for August first after meteorological experts had predicted favorable weather conditions for that date over most of the continents and a glorious day in New York, where the event would have its greatest impact and be witnessed by the President. Obviously, a celebration of this order ought to be observed on the same day in every city and hamlet throughout the world, but unfortunately the time lag made it impossible for the scientists to synchronize it.

The weather experts had made no mistake. A limpid sky illumined the old United Nations building as Fawell, chief executive of the first world government, came out, escorted by a group of officials, and after pausing for photographers, entered the limousine that would take him to the parade.

The world government, now in operation for several months, had faced a housing problem at the start. After some hesitancy, the United Nations building, emptied in short order of its incompetent tenants and useless, dust-gathering archives, had been selected as temporary headquarters, pending construction of a stately edifice worthy of housing the brain and heart of the world, the plans for which Fawell had already commissioned. Everyone agreed that New York was the choice site, with its superb, worldwide communications facilities and the traditionally international character of its citizenry and life style.

Perhaps the most surprising facet of the scientific revolution was its fast, easy success, leaving its sponsors to struggle prematurely with a host of unanticipated details. Mrs. Han had been right: in this dawn of the twenty-first century, nearly all heads of state were tired of governing, frustrated by their own fruitless efforts to solve problems beyond their competence, and this sense of frustration filtered down through the public. The Nobel letter was timely; the facts it presented, compelling. The prestige of the Nobels and their united front (internal conflicts having been screened from the public) made an overwhelming impression. Ultimately, their efforts to eliminate national secrets by removing scientific barriers dealt national leaders a mortal blow. Nearly every one resigned; odd resisters eventually were compelled to do so by the sweeping tide of public opinion.

Fawell had won the competition with a brilliant paper. Yranne and Betty Han tied for second place. In fact, at first the mathematician's essay was graded a fraction higher than the psychologist's, but the board adopted O'Kearn's view that she deserved that fraction of a point for having elected to verify the condition of the envelope containing the exam questions and not to trust anyone, including Nobels. That kind of audacity revealed strength of character, a significant factor in a test designed to uncover talent for leadership. As the astronomer Zarratoff was fourth, the Scientific World Government's promoters became its principal members, and justly so. Fawell was allowed to choose his vice-president. He hesitated, but finally took Yranne, whose clear thinking and mathematical eye for simplification he admired; Yranne would prove a valuable asset in reorganizing the world. He promised himself to consult Betty regularly on matters calling for subtle psychological insight.

Immediately after his appointment he began implementing his own program. It started out fairly well, but more slowly than he had anticipated. Instead of open hostility, an attitude of general apathy seemed to be holding things up, and it worried him. When Yranne could not offer a cure, he talked to Betty.

"Lack of enthusiasm," was her instant diagnosis. "I warned you, remember? People certainly respect Science, but they don't feel the way we do about it. Their present image of it is not exciting enough to inspire their souls or their efforts. We must try to stimulate their senses."

"I agree. We can never achieve anything grand without passion, and this is what seems to be lacking. But how do we create this excitement?"

"There are a number of very simple ways."

She mentioned several that had proved useful in her own work. Enthusiasm for world government could be aroused, she felt, by a universal anthem, a universal flag, a universal celebration with music, parades, and fireworks. These proposals were discussed in executive session and adopted, after lengthy debate, over Zarratoff's opposition to such childish antics.

As the celebration was to be worldwide, government members had traveled to key centers to preside over the ceremonies. In New York, the procession of officials, headed by Fawell, made its way directly to Science Square, the new name for Washington Square at the foot of Fifth Avenue, where the parade was to start.

All over the world other Science Squares had sprung up on historic sites, the ancient names of which had been cast aside ruthlessly: Moscow's Red Square, Place Charles de Gaulle in Paris, London's Trafalgar Square. The parades were scheduled to begin there. Each of these squares eventually would boast an imposing monument to one of the great triumphs of human endeavor. The designs had been completed, but as the celebration could not be postponed, a leafy archway, made of interwoven olive branches at the request of the peace Nobels, provided a temporary substitute.

The New York procession reached the foot of the archway. Flanked by O'Kearn and Sir Alex Keene, who insisted on standing at the President's side, Fawell laid a plain laurel wreath against a stele commemorating the martyrs of Science. Betty had suggested this ceremony to create a meditative atmosphere and prepare the public for the thrilling events in store. He stepped back as a band struck up the international anthem.

The composing of this anthem had provoked lengthy debate among members of the government. Some pointed out that an international song already existed, the "Internationale," which could easily be converted to the glory of Science just by changing a word or two. The majority felt that because the spirit of the revolution was not proletarian, it would be a mistake to adopt the song, even if some stanzas did apply, and have it awaken long-dormant sentiments which the scientists specifically wished to stifle.

So it was decided to compose a new song, but in order

to avoid confusing a public still accustomed to the accents of nationalism — and again on Betty's advice — the tune and words were based on old anthems of defunct nations.

Fawell listened to this first public performance with mixed curiosity and apprehension. The greatest composers of the day had collaborated on the music, succeeding rather well in combining the seemingly uncombinable strains of "God Save the King," the "Marseillaise," the "Star-Spangled Banner," even the "Internationale," not to mention Thailand's "Taurasben Barami," Turkey's "Istiklal Marsi," the "Jana Mana Gana" from India, and other traditional hymns to patriotism.

The words had been the biggest problem. Originally, the scientists in charge had approved a text glorifying Science, as per their instructions, but the Nobels demanded a voice in what they considered an extremely important decision. The draft they were shown struck many of them as totally unsatisfactory. The peace Nobels wanted more emphasis on peace. The literary Nobels called it the work of a rhymester and proceeded to rewrite it, producing a text devoid of scientific ideals, which was roundly rejected. The need to make the words fit the rhythm further complicated the task.

Finally, however, something of a compromise text emerged. The eloquent opening theme from "God Save the King" appealed to the musicians because its reverent effect seemed to fit the solemn first stanza:

> Ra-di-ant u-ni-verse,
> We are thy chi-il-dren
> Thy children all.

The music then swung into the strains of the old "Internationale" to these words:

We yearn to plunge ahead, oh know-ol-ledge
We seek to pe-ne-trate thy laws
And the mys-te-ry of thy be-gin-nings
And the polestar of our faith.

Then suddenly, the rousing beat of the "Marseillaise" burst in:

Sa-a-cred con-se-cration to Sci-i-ence
Our in-spi-ration thou shalt be
Thou a-lone can give u-us ho-ope
For a world of peace and u-ni-ty
For a world of peace and u-ni-ty. . . .

As these lyrics still did not suit everyone, a committee was named to improve on them. But for this first celebration of world government, the music was fine and suitable. So Fawell observed after a quick glance at the crowd assured him that the effect was harmonious and even moving.

Reentering his limousine, he stood waving at the cheering throngs as the car slowly made its way up Fifth Avenue to the reviewing stand at Madison Square. Between smiles and gestures of greeting, he managed to cast a critical eye over the double row of new banners decking the avenue.

The issue of the universal banner had been as hotly debated as that of the anthem. Garish colors once common to flags of another era were rejected as too reminiscent of the nationalistic past. Plain white cloth symbolizing peace seemed too prosaic, unlikely to stimulate the slightest emotion. Then someone suggested a banner displaying a portrait of the scientist best personifying the ascent of human knowledge. The idea seemed to have merit, and the physicist clan instantly pounced on Einstein. Fawell approved the choice, finding no serious scientific objection. Besides, the great man had the advantage of possessing a face familiar to the average citizen. That head, with its deeply furrowed features and mane of notoriously unruly hair, could indeed fire the imagination if rendered by an artist of talent.

Alas, the proposal at once rekindled the rivalry between Nobel physicists and physiologists. In the wake of fierce arguments, the project had to be abandoned as no single name could be found to suit everyone. Fawell was obliged to give up and find another emblem.

This time Yranne, with his perfect mathematical logic, was the one to advance an acceptable solution. "We quarrel about our differences when we ought to be doing the opposite," he observed. "Now there is one point on which all scientists agree: basically, we have a common goal. The magnet of all our efforts, all our research, is truth."

A murmur of approval rose, and with it the hope of extrication from this morass.

Yranne continued, "Therefore the world banner must symbolize truth and, more important, the symbol must be immediately perceptible to the public consciousness."

"We agree on these points," the scientists replied, "but how can we imagine a symbol of truth accessible to the public senses?"

"We don't have to imagine it," Yranne told them, "it already exists. The symbol of truth for humanity is a naked woman coming out of a well."

The statement produced a long silence. Wiser for years of patient study and for having had to evaluate seemingly preposterous factors likely to turn up in the results of an experiment, the scientists would never think of rejecting *a priori* a queer proposal, no matter how outrageous it might first appear. Always to analyze content was a principle of theirs. So they thought before speaking, and having thought, were forced to conclude that this one proposal alone promised a way out of the dilemma.

"A brilliant idea because it's so marvelously simple. I detect behind it the power of abstract reasoning," O'Kearn commented when they told him about it.

Once again they consulted the Nobels, who, after covering the same intellectual ground, ended up agreeing with them. A design for the banner was submitted by a well-known artist, who chose a leading actress and famous beauty to pose for the figure. The design won unanimous and enthusiastic acceptance.

That was why Fawell now rode up Fifth Avenue between two rows of banners depicting stark naked Truth, to whom a light breeze imparted graceful, occasionally sensuous, rhythms. At this very hour, Yranne, in Moscow to conduct ceremonies there, surveyed Red Square decked with the same emblems, while Betty Han, in Paris for the same purpose, measured the effect up and down the Champs-Elysées. Fawell read faces in the crowd for a clue to how people were reacting to the new flag. His impression was that they were more astonished than thrilled. This annoyed him, but he consoled himself with the thought that it takes time to accustom people to the innovations of progress.

10

THE SIGNAL of departure for the main parades all over the world was a burst of giant rockets based close enough to the cities to make their roar audible, not to say ear-splitting, and calculated to arouse the kind of contagious public enthusiasm that calls for bringing important audio-visual devices into play.

Several peace Nobels had objected to a deafening blast reminiscent of earlier war machines, but relented on learning the symbol's true significance. The rockets were in fact deadly missiles designed not to return to earth. At the peak of their trajectory, above the atmosphere, they exploded by remote control and disintegrated. All that remained was harmless dust which gradually became diluted in the immensity of space, leaving our planet purified, relieved of just so many seeds of destruction.

A hundred of these engines were launched on the outskirts of New York City, from where one could watch white contrails fading into the sky, while a thunderous roar made the ground tremble and set certain hearts fluttering. As the din subsided, the first marchers appeared and soon reached the reviewing stand where Fawell sat alongside his daughter, who had come to join him, in company with most of the Nobels.

The first units consisted of former national academies, which continued to function individually pending unification into a single world body. At their head was the Institut de France, cutting quite a figure for itself and drawing wild cheers. For indeed the Institut was taking part in the New York ceremonies along with many other scientific bodies from faraway places. Similarly, America's most prestigious organizations were parading in Moscow and Peking; the English, in Ireland; the Israelis, in former Arab states. Fawell had arranged this in order to affirm the celebration's truly international character and the permanent removal of barriers. As a matter of fact, the French notables had been flattered and honored to appear before the head of government.

They had sent a large delegation, including not only scientists but also the entire ranks of the Académie Française and other learned academies. On first hearing of the government's declared intention to bar them from participating, the Académie promptly had raised a rumpus. Literary Nobels flew to their support; the organizers ultimately agreed grudgingly to let the Fine Arts and Literature sections be represented, owing to their modest contributions to mankind's spiritual elevation.

Hearing the cheers that hailed the contingent of French academicians, Fawell had no reason to regret his decision. How dignified they looked in their dashing green uniforms with gold braid, their bicornes, and the swords (they fiercely insisted on carrying them in defiance of certain protests) which added a picturesque touch, stirring the hearts of nostalgic fanciers of old-time military parades. They marched in close order behind the permanent secretary, who dipped his bicorne with consummate grace as they passed the reviewing stand. A band was playing tunes not unlike the old military marches. If their visible efforts to keep the beat by breaking into a kind of quickstep were not entirely successful, their intentions at least were roundly applauded by the crowd.

Silently observing a great many things, Fawell noticed that throughout the ceremony the uniformed notables drew far more attention from the public than anyone else.

The parade stretched out for two hours. After the most eminent academies came the local ones, then various associations, laboratory research personnel, and finally different technical groups with close scientific affiliations, among which were cosmonauts from a number of countries, including the Soviet Union. In the front ranks Ruth fondly recognized Nicholas Zarratof, who had just arrived the night before without their having yet seen each other. She smiled and blew him a private kiss.

Each unit performed an important ceremony, the symbolic meaning of which was apparent. Two flag-bearers, one carrying the new banner, the other, the old national flag, preceded each unit as it was about to pass in review. Just before reaching the platform, the second bearer turned aside to toss the offending emblem into a ditch, which was nearly full by the end of the parade, when another ceremony took place.

A public safety unit directed the crowd to step back. Gasoline was sprinkled over the ditch; a torch was handed to Fawell, who came forward alone to toss it in. He drew back quickly as the flames shot up, then returned to the platform to stand at attention. Bearers of the new world flag formed a great circle around the fire, raising the nudes high above the heads of the crowd. Once again the world anthem rang out, while the President softly sang to himself its still undecided lyrics.

An uncertain pause followed as the flames died down; Fawell began to applaud, joined by the Nobels, and soon by the public.

Just before leaving the platform, the President gave a short speech which was broadcast worldwide. With visible emotion, he recalled events leading to the scientific revolution and the great aspirations of its government. He painted the glorious future in store for humanity, to whose service he and his ministers were dedicated. The ceremony just ended, he declared, marked the final destruction of all disgraceful barriers between nations. The speech received polite, respectful, but lukewarm, applause.

Adopting a more informal tone, he went on to excuse himself for publicly airing a private matter which, owing to its symbolic significance, he could not resist announcing on this particular day. It was his daughter Ruth's engagement to Nicholas Zarratoff, former Soviet subject, both of them now citizens of the world. Having brought the cosmonaut to the platform, the President clasped hands high in the air with the two young people, who bowed to the crowd. At this point the applause grew noticeably warmer.

Not until nightfall, however, did the enthusiasm predicted by Mrs. Han finally manifest itself on earth. For the celebration was not over yet. The parade had been merely a prelude; the psychologist's fondest hopes were vested in the ceremonies to come. Fireworks were the main attraction, a series of displays released simultaneously in the planet's zones of darkness, record numbers and varieties of rockets, creating by degrees a spectacular riot of color in the sky.

In beauty and grandeur, the finale surpassed everyone's wildest dreams, a truly universal and scientific climax which the whole world, told merely to expect a surprise, awaited breathlessly.

It began in New York with a roar even louder than the one at the start of the parade. Another burst of rockets, much larger ones this time, hurled their charges far above the atmosphere, beyond terrestrial gravity. And the charges hurtling thus into the night were the deadliest atomic bombs ever made. Americans and Russians had supplied most of them, but every nation possessing atomic power had elected to contribute a bomb as a means of reducing its own lethal stockpiles. All projectiles reached the same altitude almost simultaneously, thus stippling (for the angels) an immense spherical zone enveloping the earth's dark regions. Having ascertained that no noxious fallout would result, Fawell pressed a button to set off the local finale.

A blinding flash produced by concurrent explosions of hundreds of blazing pinwheels illumined the sky, creating a stupendous aurora borealis, while another thunderous crash announced a second wave, then a third, of similar rockets leaping into space to prolong this inspiring climax.

There and then, Nicholas and Ruth, dining in the rooftop restaurant of a skyscraper where the lights suddenly went out, as they did all over the city in order not to mar the majesty of the blazing cosmos, exchanged passionate kisses mingled with tears of joy and exhilaration. Then and there, public excitement cast off its previous restraint and churned through the city, spreading across the globe at the speed of earth's rotation, wherever similar fiery spectacles were touched off as each new zone of night came into being. Then and there, frenzied shrieks sent quivers through the earthly atmosphere. Bands of celebrants began roaming the streets, singing, rummaging through cellars and attics in search of any erstwhile national flags that might still be around. A rash of bonfires sprang up in the cities and in the countryside, prolonging far into the night the sensational display of pyrotechnics that heralded a new era. Then and there, men, women, and children, conscious of being united at last in one great family, citizens of the world, governed by wisdom and reason, bound for unprecedented glory, danced until dawn in every public square to the strains of impromptu orchestras, while glowing fires, endlessly consuming fresh piles of flags, sent up ruddy billows to sway the nudes on the world banners.

11

Betty Han had not been wrong in predicting human behavior, based on her experience of it. With orchestral skill and the aid of highly artificial devices frowned upon by a peevish minority, the August first celebration accomplished its purpose — to touch the nerve fibers of mankind. The emotion thus stimulated was effective and lasting. People suddenly felt a passionate urge to change the world, now the common homeland, and their enthusiastic efforts speeded Fawell's program on its way. It should also be said that members of the government, chosen for their scientific abilities, proved just as expert at reorganizing the superficial world as they had at penetrating its remotest strata, and as realistic about their decisions and actions as about their speculations, in contrast to the dire anticipations of this same peevish minority. Especially Vice-President Yranne, who turned in a remarkable performance in his new office. Owing chiefly to his brilliant mind and infallible instinct for getting to the root of things, the physical reorganization of the world was completed nearly on schedule, that is, in three years.

In fact, in reporting to the Nobels at the end of three years, the government could boast the following achievements:

The concept of world citizen was firmly lodged in everyone's mind. The woeful delusions of nationalism had vanished.

War was now an impossibility. Armed strength consisted of a police force under government control, employed solely — and then with utmost discretion — to maintain public order; its use was dwindling.

The world's population had been stabilized, permitting rational exploitation of resources without waste and without want.

Famine and common hunger were things of the past. As Fawell had foreseen, the surplus in certain regions and the profusion of available transport had resolved all emergencies in a matter of weeks. His agricultural innovations subsequently ruled out all such crises once and for all. With partial irrigation, the Sahara and certain Asian deserts became fertile.

Everyone was suitably housed, under ideal sanitary conditions and with all desirable conveniences.

Economic crises were over and done with now that production, trade, and exchange were centrally controlled and balanced in the interests of all the people.

The chief result of this, and the key to future operations, was a substantial reduction in the amount of work required of human beings, owing to the centralization and coherent organization of industry and agriculture, and to increased scientific and technical proficiency that allowed machines to perform all menial labor. The average two-hour work day sufficed to assure everyone a comfortable living, and promised to become even shorter.

With these physical problems out of the way and Nobel approval ringing in his ears, Fawell decided it was time to attack the second phase of his program, the spiritual domain, to which no serious attention had yet been given. The beginning ought to involve what Wells termed "sublimation of interest," the first stages of ascent, anticipating that glorious upward leap into Teilhard's noosphere.

Realistically, taking into account the obstacles along the path he had traced for humanity, and determined to overcome them by degrees, Fawell called this stage "universal scientific awareness." More than ever, he felt that everyone must work together to attain the ultimate objective, a scientific understanding of the mysteries of the Universe. More than ever, he was on guard against that hazardous reef so wrily charted in the futuristic literature of an earlier era — the division of mankind into two classes, the intelligentsia and everyone else; the latter doomed to perform crude, utilitarian labor; the former confined to an ivory tower far too slender to permit full spiritual development.

His first step was to establish a central organ of public education, never before attempted except in limited, dreadfully deficient forms, invariably favoring a microscopic elite at the expense of the many.

The government, which gave solid backing to executive aims, was convened to decide on a name for this agency. As the majority wanted to call it the World Department of Education, that name was about to be adopted when Mrs. Han asked for the floor.

"It would make more sense to call it the World Department of Leisure. We want to educate people, but we must do it tactfully. Certainly we have delivered them from the tyranny of toil; they recognize and appreciate this progress. Certainly it is only proper that they devote to scientific studies a portion of those precious hours wrenched from utilitarian labor. But should we give the impression that our sole purpose in winning them this leisure time was to put them to work at something else? Education must appear attractive."

"Still, what we actually want is to contribute that leisure to Science," Zarratoff protested.

Yranne agreed, but Fawell supported Betty, whose judgment in the subtle realm of psychology he respected.

"I think she's right," he said. "People must become aware of their freedom. Then, little by little, of their own free will, they will seek Science. I vote for the World Department of Leisure."

The others finally followed suit, and the World Department of Leisure was born. They decided to divide it into two sections, Education and Games. This last designation also came from Betty; she won acceptance for it over opposition from Yranne and especially Zarratoff, whose physical revulsion to the word "games" dated from that evening when he had had the imprudence to turn to television for relaxation. Yranne and he maintained that any scientific government worthy of that name ought to aim at gradually eliminating such infantile entertainments that already claimed too much of the public's time and distracted it from cultural pursuits.

"Games are indispensable," Betty replied. "You must admit that the sporting instinct is still very much alive; we can't afford to ignore it or not to make some concessions to it, at least in the beginning. You do play chess, don't you?"

The astronomer shrugged his shoulders, muttering that he could see no comparison between the complex movements of chess, involving a high degree of intelligence, and the triviality of ordinary amusements. But there again Fawell sided with Betty, and the government went along.

That was how the two sections of the World Department of Leisure came to be. The Education section received enormous funds, in keeping with its uncommonly ambitious objective. To Games, however, which the scientists as a whole considered secondary, they allotted a very small staff and budget. On this last point also, Betty Han had other ideas and explained them to her listeners. But now her warnings fell on deaf ears. Undeterred, she declared simply that one day they might regret not having heeded the lessons of psychology.

1

Fawell found in his morning mail a report from Zaratoff in France. Handing over everything else to his secretary, he began to read it eagerly, alone in the president's office.

For two years now, the Department of Leisure had been engaged in educating mankind, but the immensity of the task made it impossible to assess the results in so short a time.

A vast network of scientific culture encircled the globe. Imposing institutions had sprung up everywhere, with lecture halls numerous and spacious enough to seat by rotation entire urban and suburban populations on one day, and with libraries containing thousands of copies of everything needed by man to elevate his mind, from introductory science to the latest and most complex theories.

These learning centers also provided ample study rooms with microfilms, projectors, and television, encouraging users to familiarize themselves with the myriad aspects of the Universe. In laboratories equipped with the latest instruments, students could conduct private atomic experiments, induce fission for themselves, watch the magical swirl of particles through betatrons and cyclotrons, and employ highly refined devices to measure intervals of a few billionths of a second between the birth and death of certain mesons.

Education's budgetary requirements were Gargantuan. With all the riches of the globe at its disposal, the government still had had to perform new feats of ingenuity and organization to provide the necessary funds. But the purpose justified the effort, and top experts had come up with the solutions.

Needless to say, the central ingredient had not been overlooked: an army of highly competent professors, instructors, and assistants recruited to serve the student body. Some of the faculty were forced to interrupt important research, but they accepted this, having been persuaded by Fawell that their most urgent task, indeed their sublime duty, was to hand on their learning to others so that all mankind, transformed into a garden of budding scientists, could attain its destiny. As the ranking experts were government officials who could not be spared from their functions, the President decided that they could make periodic visits instead to the new centers as advisers and inspectors and, at the same time, give one or two inspiring lectures in their own special fields.

Zarratoff was doing that in France at one of the leading institutes for astronomical study. Fawell had asked him to send a private report as soon as possible, and this is what he was about to read avidly.

The beginning dealt with the center's physical design and study programs. Zarratoff found little to criticize about either. There, as everywhere else, great efforts had been made to facilitate study conditions for the hordes of students arriving every day, sometimes from remote areas. A coordinated system of trains, planes, and helicopters provided rapid, dependable transportation that operated flawlessly. Educational equipment was plentiful and of excellent quality. Several observatories with powerful telescopes and the latest optical instruments enabled students to gaze at distant planets, photograph them, analyze their spectra, and capture the concert of waves perpetually emanating into space from mysterious, at times invisible, celestial bodies. Teachers and their assistants were able and diligent.

Skipping over this already familiar record of achievement, Fawell began to frown at the next section. Zarratoff had this to say:

"Right from the start, however, it struck me that the results we anticipated were not satisfactory. There is no passionate interest in Science. Ordinary interest remains faint; the urge to know is not yet in evidence. People come to the center; they attend lectures; they sit in the library and browse through books; they watch films; they peer into telescopes. But they act as if they are carrying out orders, as if they want to avoid notice or blame for something, not as if they really want to learn. Some of the faculty have said the same thing. After speaking to a number of students, I realized that they are not assimilating their work. A few of them manage to memorize whole sections of material without any apparent understanding of its content or profound significance. Ordinary curiosity is often absent. . . ."

"Lack of enthusiasm, as Betty would say," Fawell muttered acidly, "our worst enemy."

"So I decided to wrestle with the problem and try my own hand at awakening the spirit of scientific curosity. Were the instructors perhaps teaching over the heads of these new students? Or, on the other hand, were they reverting to the old practice of talking down to students and failing to focus their interest at the very start on essential concepts? In any event, I resolved to give two lectures on a subject which I felt was bound to stimulate everyone: the Universe, seen as an entity, its birth, its probable nature, and its eventual death.

"I have just given the first of these lectures. Leaving the most advanced topics for my next one, I was obliged to begin by supplying basic facts and demolishing certain false notions. So I described the cosmos such as we already knew it to be more than a century ago, with the aid of crude instruments and primitive reasoning. Starting with the planet Earth, I showed its location in the solar system, then went on to define the sun as a single star among billions. Next I told how these stars cluster into a nebula, our Milky Way. Using simple, striking examples, I demonstrated the vast disparity between average distances within a stellar complex and the distance between stars. I suggested the shape and principal dimensions of the Galaxy. I tell you all this to show you my general method of procedure and to explain the situation, for in fact I had encountered a good many confused notions about these basic concepts. I can assure you that I expended effort and eloquence to correct them.

"Once my audience had a clear idea of our immediate environment, I could present our Galaxy as merely a single unit among billions of more or less similar galaxies once thought to be the cells of the Universe. I went a step further to show that they form solid bands, which today are regarded as the cells of the cosmos.

"Finally — and only when I felt certain they had grasped all this — I pictured the relative motions of these cells, implying the dilation of the Universe. My first lecture closed on an image of worlds drawing apart, moving away from each other at ever-increasing speeds, and left my audience with that exalted, somewhat mysterious, and altogether arresting vision. I flatter myself that my persuasiveness and eloquence have awakened their imaginations and generated a desire to know more. . . ."

"At least one person was content with the lecture," Fawell mumbled to himself.

Yet the rest of the report seemed to prove that others besides Zarratoff thought highly of his presentation, and Fawell's expression turned more cheerful as he read:

"At the end, my audience applauded warmly; the approving whispers told me that my efforts had not been wasted. I feel certain that on many faces I detected the budding curiosity and eager interest so totally lacking before. When I called for questions, the ones they asked proved at least that they had grasped the sublime importance of the subject, if not all its fine points.

"Dear friend, tonight I must tell you that in so far as astronomy is concerned, I believe we are now on the right track and will succeed; but educators should be urged to teach with passion and vision, as I set out to do. The first fruits are encouraging; I shall try to outstrip myself next week in the second lecture and will report on it to you."

Fawell put the letter down and thought for a bit.

"Passion and vision," he murmured. "Zarratoff is right; they are the crux of education. He is a good teacher, but so many others are not. Too often they tend to minimize their subject."

After further thought he decided it was high time for the top scientific experts to take an active hand. Yranne had just gone to China for a lecture tour similar to Zarratoff's. Presidential responsibilities claimed so much of Fawell's time that he had given little thought to his own contribution. To make up for this neglect, he resolved then and there to visit a physics institute outside New York City and deliver a lecture. Deferring all routine executive matters, he set to work at once on his topic.

2

"READ THIS," Fawell said.

After receiving Zarratoff's second report an hour ago, he had asked Betty to come to his office and discuss it.

"What's the matter, Fawell?' she asked, staring at him. "You look worried. Is it less optimistic than the first one?"

"Read it," the President repeated bleakly.

Betty began reading in a low voice.

". . . I returned to the final vision of my first lecture, the expanding universe, a celestial body each molecule of which is moving away from all other molecules, each galaxy from all other galaxies, at a speed proportionate to the distance between them. I emphasized, rather dramatically, I think, the paradoxical, marvelous, almost miraculous nature of this phenomenon.

"Once I felt them to be firmly in possession of the facts, I proceeded to describe the problems currently facing us in order to expose my listeners to the august significance of them. Going backward against the flow of time, I said to them, appealing to logic, mother of creative imagination: 'If today these galaxies are all pulling away from each other, then it stands to reason that in some earlier period they were closer together. If we go back far into the past, we discover a celestial body whose molecules are not separated by vast regions of space. If we go back to the farthest reaches of the imagination, we find these archipelagos crowded together, pressing up against each other, stars crushing other stars, atoms other atoms, in a singularly confined universe so incredibly consolidated, so dense, that a cubic centimeter of this primordial magma might have weighed several hundred millions of tons.'

"With suggestive images I tried to evoke the magic of our origins. I don't see how anyone can resist the eloquence of such phenomena. As a matter of fact, there wasn't a sound in the hall. The silence, which I took for a sign of meditation, seemed to augur well, and with my forehead bathed in perspiration from the effort to convey my own excitement, I was finally convinced that the 'sublimation of interest' predicted by Wells was actually occurring under my very eyes.

"Having guided my audience back to the beginning of time, I spoke of several theories bearing the stamp of this cosmological hypothesis. Lemaître's primitive atom was one of them, and I quoted a few phrases with poetic undercurrents likely to stir my listeners. This, for instance: "The evolution of the Universe may be compared to a fireworks that has just ended. A few glowing trails, embers, and smoke. Standing on an ash heap quicker than the rest to cool down, we watch suns gradually dying out and try to reconstruct the vanished splendor of worlds in the making.'* At that moment, a thrill raced through the audience, convincing me that I had managed to stir their souls. I also told them how modern cosmologists have refined Lemaître's theory.

"Having gone back to the very beginning, I invited my listeners to reverse the notion of time and turn their imaginations to the future. I described galaxies moving apart one from the other, over and over, faster and faster, until the rapidity of their motion blocks our reception of even the faintest signal from those reaching the crucial threshold: the speed of light. In all probability, I explained, this had already happened to ninety-nine per cent of them, so that even with ideal techniques of astronomic observation and flawless instruments, we would still be able to glimpse only one per cent of the total volume of the Universe, and proportionately less every second. I paused, anguished at this thought, hoping they too would sense the dramatic urgency of our situation: Unless we make haste, unless science and technology take giant strides, there will be no more than an infinitesimal part of the Universe left for us to contemplate.

"Naturally, I related this expansion, this disequilibrium, to Einstein's brilliant theories and pictured the majestic space-time edifice he erected and the host of new ideas it engendered. I ended with the exalted image of a pulsating universe, each dilation succeeded by a contraction and eventually producing another state of record consolidation, then a new explosion marking the start of a new era and a new cycle. . . .

"The throbbing of an ethereal heart, the Heart Divine. . . . The metaphor comes from Poe's *Eureka;* I read them the final pages of it. Perhaps I ought to apologize,

* Georges Lemaître, in *Revue des questions scientifiques,* November, 1931.

but this cosmological prose poem has always given me intense excitement, undiminished by all the revolting commentaries written about it by ignorant asses, male and female, which I forced myself to summarize. Basing himself on the inaccurate knowledge of his contemporaries, ignorant of Einstein's theories and cosmic dilation, relying on partly erroneous laws of physics and on his own faulty logic, through what sorcery did Poe still manage to arrive at a concept of the Universe which today seems probable to some of our greatest experts? I left them to reflect on that paradox.

"Dear friend, I assure you that I spared no effort to instill a trace of the passion that drives us. My final words came from Einstein himself: 'The cosmic religious experience motivates the most ambitious and the noblest scientific experiments.'

"That was my final flourish. It left me exhausted, but confident and optimistic. However . . ."

"So far I don't see what you have to complain about," Betty commented. "An excellent lecture, masterful, I venture to say, though stamped with a certain mysticism. But then we know Zarratoff has the soul of a poet. In any case, it doesn't seem to conflict with our aims. What do you object to?"

"Object to? Nothing at all. It's excellent, as you said, and thoroughly eloquent. Why, Betty, I was thrilled from start to finish, even though the bulk of it was familiar to me. Most of our colleagues would feel the same way."

"Didn't his audience?"

"Finish reading," Fawell said wearily.

"However," Zarratoff's report continued, "I am obliged now to tell you about a rather painful incident that gave me an unpleasant feeling. I had left the lecture hall, which was packed to the rafters, in a burst of applause — sincere, I can assure you. All eyes were sparkling. In two three-hour lectures I could pride myself on having revitalized the mood of the institute. My optimism was reinforced a half hour later when, having rested and caught my breath, I made my way to the reception room to meet a delegation from the lecture hall. I had told them that I would gladly answer any questions they might have.

"As I could not handle a large crowd, I had asked them to collect the questions and have one or two delegates present them to me. About a dozen came, representing probably the entire student body. They all seemed impatient to see me.

"I complimented them on their eager curiosity while observing them closely. As far as I could tell, they came from all classes of the former society: workers, employers, housewives, society women, ranging in age from sixteen to sixty. I welcomed the diversity. Their faces seemed to convey a mixture of ardor and anxiety which I attributed to the mental strain of contemplating the new perspectives I had revealed, and to fear of missing some vital detail or stumbling into error. . . ."

"I remember that state of mind from my student days," Betty commented.

"Zarratoff has known it too, otherwise he couldn't talk about it that way; the same applies to me and to lots of us," Fawell responded in a hollow voice. "Even lately this haunting obsession has kept me awake nights. Read the rest."

"The first to speak was a man about fifty years old. He seemed energetic and used to responsibility. Actually, as I found out later, he came from the managerial class and even since the revolution had been assigned important work. A logical, practical person, he had done an excellent job of coordinating transportation between various remote areas.

"He began talking to me like a bashful schoolboy: 'Sir, my question probably betrays great ignorance, but I would like to know . . .' At that point his voice wavered and broke off.

"I begged him not to feel embarrassed because curiosity, the craving for knowledge, was sufficient excuse for any blunder.

"This seemed to buoy up his courage and he went on: 'Well, you see, this question has been bothering me for ages, and the answer is probably obvious to you, sir, but I would like to know whether the reigning planet . . .'

" 'The "reigning" planet?' I repeated, aghast.

" 'It is sometimes called "legislative," ' he informed me. 'I would like to know whether the influence of the "legislative" planet in the "ascendant" is affected while in conjunction with one of myriad galaxies filling the sky which you just described so graphically.'

"Dear friend, I leave you to imagine my distress when I recovered from this stunning blow and finally realized that he was talking about horoscopes and astrology. It was the only topic of real interest to him. I didn't have a chance to reply for just then a woman, this time of humbler origin, had come charging forward and was kneeling in front of me, frantically spreading out on the floor a sheet of paper covered with diagrams which she implored me to examine to see if her 'nativity' was correct. A famous astrologer had cast it, but after hearing my lecture, she began to suspect that the sky contained more than astrologers knew and that perhaps I could read her future better and more accurately.

"The others were all of the same mind, meaning that

their heads were stuffed full of 'houses,' 'luminaries,' 'heavenly bodies in the ascendant,' 'themes,' and 'signs,' all either benevolent or malevolent. Horoscopes constituted the one and only topic that, without preconsultation, they wished to hear me expound. They all began talking at once, waving diagrams, and subjecting me to a barrage of bizarre, frantic questions concerning the same disgraceful nonsense which charlatans once used to beguile the poor with hope, thereby extending their influence over the masses, an influence which, according to my experience, has not diminished since the scientific revolution. It explains the sparkling eyes and throbbing pulses. They expected me to complete or correct the divinations of sorcerers!

"Dear friend, I leave it to you to interpret this episode as you will; tonight I am too distressed to do so myself.

"There is little to add. I tried to regain my composure and to show them how foolish they were. I advanced every unassailable argument you and I know. They listened politely without interrupting, but bit by bit I was obviously losing whatever prestige my eloquence had established. And sensing the gulf between us, I felt less persuasive. When I finished, the man who had spoken first shook his head, saying, 'Still, Mr. So-and-so *did* die in the third month of the year, just as his horoscope predicted.'

"To present him with the theory of probability would have been a waste of time. I gave up; they went away dejected, leaving me utterly crushed. . . ."

"There you are, Betty," Fawell said. "That tells you why I'm not exactly crowing."

He seemed so upset that she refrained from criticism and tried to comfort him.

"Perhaps deviations of this kind are necessary," she

suggested, then cited a remark of Kepler's: " 'Without someone's credulous hope of reading the future in the sky, would you ever have been wise enough to study astronomy for its own sake?' "

But Fawell was too depressed to let anything cheer him. "A gulf between them and us, Zarratoff says."

"After all, it's only the first boring; the next one may prove more encouraging."

"I made a second one myself," Fawell said, more grimly than ever. "I also gave a lecture, and on a vast subject, the structure of matter and its unity. I won't repeat it for you, but you may be certain that, like Zarratoff, I put every ounce of energy into stimulating at least interest, if not passion . . . a classic lecture, to which I added a bit of zest by describing the principal divisions of matter, molecules and atoms, and ultimately its unity, reduced in the final analysis to uniformly identical particles. They understood this last point — and how! Again like Zarratoff, I offered to answer questions afterwards and was pleased to be approached by a sizable delegation. Can you guess the one question they asked me — the only one?"

"Depressing, no doubt."

"How to make gold!" Fawell bellowed. "Don't you see? Since all bodies eventually reduce to the same physical properties, I'm supposed to possess a simple, handy recipe, no doubt requiring only a retort and burner, for transmuting beach pebbles or unwanted garden stones into gold."

Once again the psychologist tried to be encouraging. "At least it proves they understood something about the unity of matter. And perhaps superstition is also a stage that can't be bypassed. I think —"

The telephone rang. It was Yranne calling the President from Peking. Fawell listened to him in silence for quite some time. He made no comment when Yranne finished, simply saying, "All right, we'll discuss that in our next conference."

But when he turned to Betty, his face looked wearier than ever. For a while he said nothing.

"May I ask how my former countrymen are doing?" she finally inquired.

"He lectured on statistics and probability," Fawell said haltingly, "emphasizing their importance in daily life as well as in the Universe."

"And?"

"Again, only one question came up afterwards. You can't imagine what it was."

"With a look at your face and a little effort, I can probably make a good guess," Betty replied coolly.

Fawell slammed his fist on the table in a burst of rage. "They asked him — they implored him on bended knee to show them an infallible system for winning at roulette!"

3

WHEN SEVERAL tours of inspection in various parts of the world failed to produce more favorable results, the education of mankind became an issue of grave concern to the world government. Its members soon had plenty of other problems on their hands in connection, oddly enough, with persons who seemed to be progressing in the right direction, who cherished scientific development and who, in gratitude for their deliverance from slavish toil, were profiting from their new freedom and leisure by cultivating their minds. That was the very path recommended by the world administration. Yet among those people were discovered one day the symptoms of a strange disorder.

The first victim available for observation was Nicholas Zarratoff, Fawell's own son-in-law, now a veteran astronaut who had welcomed the scientists' revolution and was enjoying its effects. Before him, however, two fatal accidents had alarmed the authorities as the victims were also space pilots who died under identical, baffling conditions. The first man, Jim Barley, was piloting his own plane on leave. An allegedly peculiar conversation had been in progress between himself and the control tower at the airport where he was scheduled to land. Unfortunately, this conversation had not been recorded and sounded so incoherent as to suggest that the employee reporting it had suffered a lapse of memory. He claimed that Barley said he was unable to land the plane on his own, though it was operating normally and the visibility was perfect. The employee never found out why because the airman's desperate efforts to explain himself became unintelligible. The incident ended tragically. The plane suddenly lurched out of control and crashed. Barley's body was recovered in the twisted wreckage; an investigation turned up nothing.

The WAO (World Astronautics Organization) inferred some sort of seizure, and the incident would have been closed if a similar accident had not befallen a second astronaut just a few days later while he too was piloting a pleasure craft. Like Barley, he had begun to mutter incomprehensibly and died in the same manner. The WAO's perplexed doctors wondered what kind of illness could have claimed the two victims, and none of the psychologist consultants could produce a convincing diagnosis. The two successive accidents seemed unusual enough to warrant a confidential report to the government.

Nicholas Zarratoff was glad to be alive that morning, with the prospect of a three-month vacation just granted him. He had earned it, and now at last he could take Ruth on the extended honeymoon they had been planning for so long and forever postponing each time an urgent assignment called him away.

Leaving the office where he had just learned the good news, he leaped into his car and raced home, forgetting the speed limit. Ruth was cutting flowers in the garden; he embraced her passionately.

"I've got it!" he shouted joyously. "Three months!"

"Three months, darling? I thought . . ."

"Three whole months. The two coming to me for the mission and a month extra for . . ."

"For what?"

Ruth stared at him anxiously. A frown seemed to hover on his face, then quickly disappeared as he replied with somewhat forced gaiety, "It's a present from the WAO's medical board. They really outdid themselves."

"You're not sick, are you, dear?"

"Never felt better in my life. But after the checkup and all the tests they put me through, they seem to think . . . I really don't know what it's all about; neither do they, I fancy . . . anyway, they seem to think they found something that might indicate a slight sign of mental instability. . . . Just that vague. So they all agreed that an extra month's vacation wouldn't do any harm. That's the whole story."

"Are you worried?"

"Worried!" He burst out laughing, swept her into his arms and whirled her around. "Don't you see, it's their way of thanking me for all my work these past few years. The medic who read me the report just shrugged it off with a laugh. Who knows, maybe your presidential parent gave secret orders to the WAO to let us get away for a long honeymoon. Worried? I tell you I've never felt better or happier. When do we leave?"

"The day after tomorrow if you like. I don't need more

than two days to pack. . . . And we've known where we're going for a long time."

"Fine. I'll whip over to the airport and check over old *Icarus.*"

That was the name of his private plane. A former test pilot, he had received it as a farewell gift from his employer companies when he switched to space flights. Each time he came back from a mission, he would use it for short excursions with Ruth. He kept the plane mainly for a long trip around the world.

After checking *Icarus* over and finding it in good order, he gave final instructions to the mechanics and returned to help his wife.

He was about to garage the car when a trivial incident upset him. Like the rest of the house, the garage was equipped with the latest labor-saving devices. Nicholas had had a variety of gadgets installed, some designed by him as he enjoyed fiddling around with such projects. An electric eye raised and lowered an iron grill at the garage entrance; an approaching car would cut off a beam of light, causing the grill to rise. With practice, he had so perfected the timing of his approach, once calculated but now instinctive, that the front end of the car slid into the garage just under the rising grill.

But this time it didn't work. The grill stayed down, and Nicholas began behaving strangely. He sat there staring at the entrance, his hands gripping the wheel, his foot still pressing down on the gas pedal while the car continued to roll forward. The sight of the approaching obstacle made him feel helpless, paralyzed by a kind of panic. The torpor lasted three or four seconds; just as the car was about to hit the grill he suddenly snapped out of it and slammed on the brake.

Stepping out of the car, he felt uneasy at first about

the strange feeling he had experienced, then violently hostile to the defective mechanism, a rage far out of proportion to such a trivial incident. It took several minutes to regain control of himself, raise the grill manually, and bring the car into its stall. Even then he had difficulty coordinating his movements and made several passes before finally maneuvering the car alongside Ruth's.

Calm again, he stood motionless for a while, brooding over the uncertain findings in his medical report. Then he shrugged, forced himself to concentrate on preparing for the trip, and when he rejoined his wife, his face was serene once more.

The WAO differed from its ancestor NASA and from related organs which it had assimilated both as to its facilities, tenfold more generously endowed, and its choice of priorities, which consistently reflected strictly scientific criteria. No longer was there any question of winning a race or a wager by sending a handful of men to spend a few hours on the moon and bring back a pile of rocks. In this domain as in all others, the true science was meant to be served. A rational exploration of space implied that teams of experts and all necessary equipment should be installed on accessible heavenly bodies in order to study them systematically.

As a corollary of this policy, the first fruits of space probes were profoundly significant but not spectacular. It had taken time to orchestrate the programs of former nations which differed widely both as to objectives and modalities. A station the size of a small city was now orbiting the earth, making lunar voyages a routine affair. The moon, still the unique astral conquest, was in the planning stage, with observatories and permanent laboratories already installed. The space station eventually would serve as a departure point for flights to other planets. Exploration of Mars was projected in the near future. At present several space ships had circled it, bringing back a mass of information for use in organizing the expedition.

Nicholas Zarratoff had led one of these last flights, which had kept him in space for several months. Ruth had urged him to accept the assignment, a major event of his career, for which he had been selected. He deserved the honor as much for his extensive space experience and steady nerves as for his prompt, dependable reactions. In an era when mechanical equipment was still subject to failure, he had jumped in on several occasions, like the first moon pioneers, to take over the controls and correct a critical situation beyond the competence of any computer.

Actually, there had been no call for him to react spontaneously for quite some time and probably never would be again. Mechanical failures had been so rare in the last three years that they now could be regarded as virtually impossible miracles. The WAO had outlawed accidents in behalf of the eminent passengers these spacecraft now carried, all famous scientists. The safety standards applied to every piece of equipment called for not just the 98–99 percent reliability operative in the past, but for 99,999,999 . . . stretching over a whole row of nines. To Nicholas Zarratoff and to other veteran astronauts, mechanical failures belonged to the remote past. As for the younger generation of spacemen, the possibility of an on-board computer going awry would strike them as a joke. They would find equally farfetched the notion of any defect in the colossal ground organization monitoring their flight, watching everything, anticipating everything, feeding them a constant stream of instructions.

During the last flight around Mars the equipment had functioned impeccably as usual, and Commander Zaratoff had not had the slightest cause for alarm in all those long months. Computers controlled and monitored the trajectory at every instant. When a split-second decision needed to be made, the spaceship's computers made it. They were more sensitive and quicker to respond than any pilot; they could register the problem, find the solution, and order the proper responses before a human brain could even begin to react. In such cases the powerful heavy artillery of ground computers never even came into play, for communications between a ship in the vicinity of Mars and the earth would take several minutes. It operated only when a problem could wait that interval or longer for solution.

In time, Nicholas came to rely on them entirely; this left him long periods of idleness inside the spacecraft. He used the time to study and to broaden his scientific knowledge with the help of eminent scientists on board. They became willing instructors, offering courses to meet the needs of the commander and several of the crew, who were also relieved of the constant strain of former responsibilities. On this voyage, guided by impeccable electronic brains, the spaceship reached its appointed destination without straying as much as an inch off course.

4

RUTH FINISHED packing on schedule and the couple took off in *Icarus* on a sunny morning, which they took for the sign of a happy trip ahead.

After shaking hands with the ground crew and a few friends who had come to see them off, they climbed aboard and Nicholas took the controls. He had not piloted the plane for several months. The day before he had taken it out for a practice ground run just to get the feel of it again. Flying a pleasure craft like this one was child's play for a former test pilot. Besides, *Icarus* had all the latest equipment for continuous ground-to-air communications and for blind landing.

Even before takeoff Nicholas contacted several control posts to confirm that everything was in order and weather conditions good along his course. Then he smiled at Ruth, kissed her lovingly, taxied to the edge of the runway, gunned the motors and took off.

The astronaut base they had left behind was in the Sahara, which experts had found to be an excellent launching place for heavy missiles. Nicholas had been stationed there while it was being built shortly after the advent of world government. Ruth joined him at the end of a two-year engagement and they were married. He had shared then in the birth and development of what was to become a major world center, witnessing at the same time with eager eyes the creation of canals and lakes which altered the local climate radically. He knew the region like the palm of his hand, having flown over it and driven around it during vacations.

The trip would take them over the former desert to Morocco for a long stay; then across the Atlantic (*Icarus* had undergone certain alterations to extend its radius of action), after which, in short hops, they would cover the whole American continent. The itinerary included stopping over for several days to see their parents, Fawell and Zarratoff, in the New York area where the government was now permanently housed. Afterwards they planned to head for Canada, Asia, and the European mainland.

The first lap of the flight, about three hours, was uneventful. They marveled at the Sahara, now transformed into vast expanses of green etched with tiny canals, then flew over a straight stretch of railway bordering a main canal much larger than the others and slicing the plain with two parallel lines converging at the horizon. Following this ideal landmark would bring them straight to their first stop, a small recently built village where friends were expecting them. Ruth found the flight delightful; it was her first long excursion in years.

For no apparent reason, she suddenly became aware of a strange feeling in the cockpit. The weather was still perfect, they were cruising through limpid skies, but her contentment had vanished. It took her a moment to trace the unpleasant sensation to a change in her husband's behavior. Nothing really abnormal, only at first he had talked to her on and off. . . . More important still, he had turned to look at her each time and smile. Now he hadn't done that for . . . several minutes at least, and maybe much longer. It was this absence of contact that worried her.

She looked at him. His position at the controls was normal . . . or maybe not completely so. Examining him more carefully, she thought he seemed strangely rigid. Or tense. Yet flying this plane usually was sheer fun for him.

"Is everything all right, darling? Are you tired?"

She had asked the question almost against her own will. He replied, but after a slight pause and without looking at her. His voice sounded strangely distant.

"No, everything's fine. Except . . . excuse me. . . ." He was putting in a call to a nearby station. On contact, he asked in distinctly anxious tones, "Did your radar pick me up?"

"One moment please, Mr. Zarratoff," said a voice tinged with respect.

In aeronautics circles he was something of a celebrity both for his space exploits and for being the President's son-in-law.

"Yes, there you are. You must be over the railway line, heading our way."

At the pilot's request, the man on the ground gave him his speed and approximate distance from the station as best he could gauge them.

"Please give me a better distance reading," Nicholas instructed him imperiously.

"About seven miles," replied the voice, tinged with surprise. "You must be nearly on top of the stone bridge."

"About! . ." the astronaut began. Ruth gave a start. His voice had an angry edge, entirely uncalled for. Just as suddenly his composure returned, and he said, with apparent relief, "Yes, that's right, of course, I'm flying over the stone bridge. I recognize it."

"You couldn't miss it if you tried," came the voice, now sarcastic.

As a matter of fact, the bridge was the only one of its kind in Africa, the work of a slightly demented engineer who had dismantled stone by stone an ancient European bridge several centuries old and reassembled it here. Upon learning of this eccentric feat, the authorities first resolved to demolish it but finally allowed it to stand as a curiosity and built a second, more modern and solid, bridge not far away. No one could possibly mistake the old one.

"Need anything else, Mr. Zarratoff?"

"Please! Just a moment! Don't cut me off!"

Ruth was panic-stricken. He had all but screamed, his voice nearly frantic. She had never heard him talk that way.

"Something wrong on board?"

"No, everything's all right. I just want to check. . . . Will you give me my exact altitude?"

"Is your altimeter off?"

"I'm not sure . . . anyway, it's not a precision instrument. I have more faith in your radar."

"Seventy-five hundred feet."

The aircraft carried the same reading. Once again the pilot appeared relieved. Yet he went on talking as if desperately anxious not to be cut off, or so it seemed to Ruth.

"Will you give me my exact course?"

After this was done, he asked a most peculiar question in those circumstances. "Will you track me on your radar screen?"

The voice on the ground registered stupefaction and asked to have the sentence repeated, which Nicholas did with fresh impatience.

"Say, Mr. Zarratoff, you're asking us to monitor you, right? Of course we can do it. But you're only about sixty-five hundred feet up. The weather is ideal, the visibility excellent. There isn't a cloud from here to your next stop and your course is a straight line parallel to the railway and the canal."

"That's true," Nicholas murmured. "I have the railroad tracks and the canal."

The last few words trailed off almost to a mumble. The voice asked once more, "You're sure everything's all right up there?"

"Everything's fine. Plane and pilot are fine."

"And you still want radar guidance?"

"No, never mind. I can follow the railroad tracks."

"Well, good-bye then, Mr. Zarratoff, and bon voyage."

"Good-bye."

He hung up the phone. Calmer now, he smiled at Ruth, who had not uttered a word during the entire dialogue.

"Why all the questions, dear?" she ventured, after a pause. "We couldn't possibly get lost in such fine weather. I recognize the countryside below. There's the old town right off the highway. We drove there just after we were married. There's the hotel where we stayed, and the swimming pool."

It was true, and Nicholas knew the area even better than she. "You can't be too careful," he offered solemnly.

It wasn't like him at all. At that moment she too thought of the medical board's vague reservations and wondered if he were seriously ill. Disguising her anxiety, she said gaily, "We'll be there in twenty minutes. The Hudsons are probably waiting for us already."

They were the friends who had offered to put them up for the night. Hudson was manager of the airport.

Nicholas did not answer. Having tried unsuccessfully for the last few moments to contact the airport, he began to show fresh signs of nervousness. "It's sheer madness the way they let a plane wander around the sky without keeping tabs on it," he muttered. "I'll make a complaint."

They glided on through the limpid air. Ruth did not dare say a word and both remained silent for some time. But Nicholas seemed to grow edgier as they approached the airport.

"We must be almost there," she said at last.

He did not answer but stared straight ahead, never glancing down at the field below. And he was still at the same altitude, which also surprised her. She had flown enough to know that by now he ought to have begun his descent. She was about to say so when he finally made contact with the ground. At once he began pouring out strange questions: How far away was he? What altitude? Should he begin his descent? At what angle? When the answers finally came after some delay, his friend Hudson was on the wire.

"That's a good one! You recognized my voice? Anyone else would have taken you for an idiot."

"I'm not joking," said Nicholas. "Should I come down?"

Hudson gathered from the tone of Zarratoff's voice that he certainly was not joking. "Well, of course. At least if you intend to eat with us tonight. But you'll have to circle a bit before landing. I can spot you clearly. You're right above us."

"Right above?"

"Can't you see the runways?"

"Right above . . . right above," Nicholas repeated mechanically.

In fact Ruth could pick out every detail of the airport, runways, control tower, hangars. But her husband still had not glanced down even once. He seemed distraught.

"All right, I'm going down," he murmured hesitantly.

When there was no response from below, Nicholas flew into a rage. "Well, what in God's name are you waiting for? Give me my position, angle, course, altitude, at every second, every second, d'you hear me. . . . Can't you bring me in by radar?"

"If it weren't you, I'd swear the pilot was stone drunk," said Hudson. "The runway is in full sun."

"The sun . . . the sun . . ."

Hudson finally realized that there was something drastically wrong. "Nicholas, are you ill? Answer me."

But Nicholas was incapable of answering. All he could do was look helplessly at his wife and murmur, "They're deserting us, darling. I don't know what to do."

5

THAT DAY Fawell was meeting with Vice-President Yranne to discuss a situation that was eating his heart out. He had asked Betty to join them, knowing that the frustrating business of trying to educate mankind was demanding increased psychological expertise.

Only a tiny minority was making progress; the majority remained apathetic, or recalcitrant, or absorbed in pursuits totally inconsistent with scientific ideals.

"We may be guilty of self-deception," the President began solemnly. "We are not on the right track. Despite all our efforts, the majority has no interest in rudimentary learning. If this continues, it will produce the very thing we want to avoid. Mankind will tend to be split into two categories: on the one hand, a caste of educated, privileged leaders like ourselves; on the other, an apathetic populace that will have to be kept busy at unskilled labors, identical, happy in their own way perhaps, but never to experience the pure joys of the mind, just so much dead weight on the march to progress. And it can only get worse."

"Allow me, if you will, to be even more pessimistic than yourselves," Betty Han interjected. "If my analysis of the current situation is correct, we find no 'sublimation of interest.' Instead we find deviation — hazardous deviation — with the result that the masses threaten to act as a powerful brake, far worse than a dead weight."

"How well I know it," Fawell growled. "Don't you think I saw it happening?"

What Betty meant was the alarming fact that even if the people of the world were not precisely bent on cultivating their minds by acquiring the secrets of Science, they were becoming increasingly absorbed in the material rewards of scientific discoveries, to the point of forever insisting on more substantial and more refined products. These mounting demands, odd at times but consistently imperative, threatened to block the Scientific World Government's noble aims.

"Today the Eskimos are demanding larks!" Yranne sighed.

Now that hunger had been banished from the earth, once-starving populations were no longer content with a scientifically balanced diet. They wanted an ever-expanding choice of delicacies and the government did its best to satisfy them. Indeed, in a world dedicated to egalitarian ideals, it seemed both unfair and unreasonable to give the temperate regions first claim to choice and delectable fresh produce and expect everyone else to make do with frozen goods. Natural science experts had helped to achieve extraordinary results in this area. Asian and African lakes, once deserts, now were stocked with new strains of the most exquisite-tasting salmon and trout, while colonies of pheasants and ortolans thrived in the new forests and green belts. By a painstaking process of selection, biologists had even succeeded in breeding new and widely adaptable varieties of sturgeon in sufficient quantity to satisfy world demand for caviar. In addition, special institutes offered monthly courses to thousands of student cooks in the art of preparing delicate sauces, once the pride of a tiny privileged minority.

Housing demands were equally insistent. Slums had been replaced long ago with up-to-date, sanitary, practical dwellings furnished with what used to be called modern conveniences. But the latter no longer suited former slum dwellers who now expected central air conditioning, a telephone and television in every room, push-button windows and awnings with bedside controls and, in general, a complete range of mechanical, electrical, and electronic devices for eliminating all physical effort.

Every family wanted its own house and swimming pool. This craving for comfort, this universal desire to possess scientific and technological achievements without understanding their essence and without having shared in the intellectual effort to discover them, did not stop at housing. To satisfy demands, whole new cities had to be built, their streets and public squares heated in winter, cooled in summer. Linking these cities called for a communications system substantial enough to avoid congestion, especially at peak hours, as well as a fleet of flying machines offering round-the-clock service to all points of the globe with numerous local landing areas to save time.

All this involved a staggering industrial output, the construction of huge factories, larger power stations, and the discovery of new energy sources. Now the physicists had to pitch in, for the government, yielding once again, would not deny any part of the population the supercomforts enjoyed by others. Unfortunately, this program implied using up large quantities of the earth's physical resources.

". . . And alienating a substantial share of its spiritual resources," Betty added emphatically, as the Big Three continued their conference.

It was true, and the truth of it was beginning to terrify Fawell. Scientists, precious instruments of thought, had to interrupt or slow down basic research projects devoted to genuine progress in order to appease humanity's insatiable appetite for comfort, luxury, and material refinements.

At this rather discouraging stage of the conference, a telephone rang in the President's office. It surprised and alarmed him as he had left instructions that he was not to be disturbed except for an extreme emergency.

Frantic over the incoherent phrases coming from Nicholas, now mingled with Ruth's pleas, Hudson had called officials at the WAO, who saw a direct connection with the two preceding accidents. Medical authorities in turn were alerted. An unprecedented telephone consultation then began among the various scientists, physicians, physiologists, and psychologists all over the world who had studied the cases of Jim Barley and the other astronaut without being able to diagnose the problem. Because of the important passengers involved, WAO's chief took it upon himself to disturb the President.

After the first few words, Fawell's face dropped. "A third case," he said in a husky voice. "This time it's Nicholas, and Ruth is with him."

He pressed a button and the voice on the other end filled the room. All three of them heard the rest of the tale. Fawell cast helpless, desperate glances at his two friends as if imploring them to do something. Yranne was silent. Betty, who had studied the first two cases professionally, remained calm as usual and was thinking.

"What is he doing right now?" she asked as soon as the caller had finished.

Recognizing Mrs. Han's voice, the chief of WAO replied, "He's circling the airport, but we can't get him to come down. Every few minutes we give him a change of course to keep him in a circle."

"Does he follow your instructions?"

"To the letter, but that's all he can do."

"Suppose you assign him an angle of descent. . . ."

"We've tried. It doesn't work. He started and gave up right away, saying he didn't dare and wanted to make an instrument landing. But there's no need for it; the visibility is perfect. . . ."

"What difference does that make?" Betty interrupted impatiently. "Go ahead and do it."

"That's what we said. I told you we tried everything, but even that doesn't work."

"Why? He gave a reason. I'd like to know the exact words he used, even if they don't make sense. It's very important. Have them repeated to you," Betty ordered imperiously.

"Consider it an executive order," Fawell broke in, hanging on Betty's words.

A pause, and the reply came: "They could only make out this much: 'I can't, I can't . . . it's seeing the runway, I tell you I can see the runway. . . .' Then some mumbled gibberish."

"How much gas does he have?"

"Plenty. His plane has an extensive radius of action, and he filled up before takeoff."

"Hold the line a moment," Betty told him. "I'm thinking."

She clamped her head between her hands while Fawell looked on in anguished silence, not daring to interrupt her thoughts. Finally she straightened up. "I have an idea, Fawell. Isn't he over a station on the edge of the Sahara? Quick, tell me. He can't be far from the outer range of the Moroccan Atlas."

"Not more than one hundred and twenty-five miles away," Yranne cut in. "I know the area."

"And in the vicinity of those mountains there must be clouds at times, and fog, right?"

Yranne eyed her fixedly for an instant, then gave a sharp cry as he caught her meaning. "And if not, we can make all we want," he exclaimed. "We have a meteorological station there which did some conclusive tests recently. . . . Fawell, let me give the orders. There isn't a second to lose."

Without waiting for the President's response, he grabbed a second phone to alert additional agencies, pouring out excited instructions.

"What's the name of your station? Is there an airport nearby? Exactly where is it?" Betty asked him.

Nodding his head, Yranne pinpointed the location for her while he waited to hear from the station. Betty picked up the first phone; Fawell, too upset to do anything, motioned to her to act as she pleased.

"This is what I want you to do," she said into the phone.

While Yranne was directing the proper agencies to produce a curtain of clouds and thunderstorms in the area, Betty gave urgent instructions to Hudson.

As a result of all these intercessions, a precise course was assigned to Nicholas, who followed it obediently and, in less than an hour, found himself in a blanket of fog. There, the station's radar system was able to pick him up and guide him to the airport where the storm had reduced visibility to zero.

Through arrangements made by a number of authorities, all communications, including air-to-ground conversations, were now being relayed to the President's office, providing him and his two colleagues with a direct line to the drama's happy ending.

They were able to observe, with understandable relief, a fact which, though singular, did not appear to surprise the psychologist. The astronaut's voice became steadier and more distinct once the plane encountered fog. And when total obscurity set in, leaving him dependent on radar guidance, he regained his normal composure, responding with customary efficiency to the automatic signals from below.

"Congratulations, Betty," Yranne said. "Your idea was sound."

Fawell simply gave her a hug and said nothing. He, too, had understood.

The blind landing in pea-soup fog was executed perfectly. When Nicholas and his tearful wife were greeted by station officials, he was unable to account for his strange behavior. To all questions his reply was the same: "I don't know what came over me."

6

OTHER CASES of this strange disorder occurred among astronauts, giving the impression at first that it affected only spacemen. The symptoms varied from benign all the way to fits of hysteria. For example, one man came down with it at the wheel of his car just as he was about to park between two other vehicles; he stopped abruptly, halfway out into the street, blocking traffic, then was heard shouting at passersby to call the WAO and find out the proper set of maneuvers. He could not function independently.

Panic threatened, on top of other governmental concerns, when it became apparent that the disorder was spreading to other social groups and in fact no one was safe. Despite the wide variety of symptoms, all cases had one common factor defined by Betty Han, who had studied them with true professional zeal, as "loss of confidence in the ego." This came to be known simply as LCE.

Up and down the social ladder LCE began to take its

toll, provoking incidents that ranged from ludicrous to tragic. The central switchboard in a major hotel, for instance, where a single employee supervised the automatic system, had its computer break down one day because of a short circuit, after performing flawlessly for several months; the woman employee, formerly an expert operator, proved incapable of sticking a plug into a hole corresponding to a certain room number and began to scream hysterically for a relief computer.

In an apartment building where, as everywhere else, a thermostat maintained temperature constancy, the superintendent could not manage to perform the simple act of pushing a button to start the boilers working one very cold day when the automatic device was damaged.

A traveling accountant, separated from the calculators to which he had grown accustomed, was at a loss to pay his hotel bill because he could not count his cash.

A singularly laughable case was that of a famous author who, after completing a major effort, a thousand-page saga, was powerless to sign the publisher's contract. He was so wedded to a dictaphone, so utterly dependent on that instrument and the services of a typist, that he had lost confidence in his ability to write. His publisher was obliged to settle for a verbal agreement and an "X."

Finally, other examples of LCE striking with tragic results, in addition to the first two cosmonauts, were numerous victims of polio. Oddly enough, this disease, unlike a long list of others plaguing the human race, had not been eliminated. The vaccine had even lost some of its potency and many persons were stricken. Fortunately, medicine had now developed a new method to remove all traces of the disease, but the treatment was slow, confining the patient to an iron lung for several months. Numerous special hospitals and excellent equipment made it possible to care for all polio sufferers and to restore ninety percent of them to health.

Well, a few patients thus treated and released as completely cured suddenly lost their ability to breathe normally. Not because of any virus or disease of the spinal cord, however, for they were in perfect physical condition, as medical examinations confirmed beyond a doubt. The diagnosis was an acute form of LCE. They had lost confidence in their ability to breathe without mechanical aid. Many of them suddenly blacked out and could not be resuscitated; others survived long enough to be rushed back into iron lungs, there to regain the serenity and stability that had forsaken them.

And while the scientific government endured crushing defeats and wrestled with bewildering problems, a new scourge descended on mankind, dispatching monstrous visions to invade Fawell's sleep. The suicide rate took an alarming leap.

Those implacable statistics sent shivers up his spine. If the upward trend continued as it had for weeks (and Yranne the mathematician saw no reason for it not to unless conditions changed radically), humanity was rushing headlong to self-destruction. An all-out effort was imperative to eliminate the causes of this disorder, but no one quite knew what they were as most suicides turned out to be acts of well-adjusted, healthy, financially unembarrassed creatures.

A scientific commission appointed to study the question ventured to postulate an epidemic of unhappy or thwarted love affairs. Subsequent investigations discredited that hypothesis. Out of a thousand suicides, only one or two could be attributed by any stretch of the imagination to frustrated passion; the rest remained a mystery defying scientific analysis.

Looking back over the achievements of his administration with the scrupulous objectivity he always brought to such analyses, Fawell was forced to conclude the following:

Even though the Scientific World Government had succeeded in reorganizing the planet systematically, and with excellent material results, its record on the spiritual level seemed haunted by failure.

Having decided this for himself, he fell into deep despair over the seemingly hopeless conflict with his ideals.

Other worries tormented him. The current situation was drawing sharp criticism in daily cabinet sessions. Rivalries, blunted at first by the pleasant experience of success, were now opening rifts among officials, and the two main groups of scientists had resumed their warring. Debates grew bitter at times, usually over the same, and for them crucial, point. The classic issues of capitalism, fascism, the proletariat, the class struggle, communism, democracy, and even socialism failed to excite them, but not the question of whether the Universe ought to be viewed and studied independent of man, the implicit or avowed position of physicists like O'Kearn and Fawell himself, or, on the contrary, as a function of man, the doctrine endorsed by all biologists. The latter had a field day attributing current setbacks to the inhumanity of physicists. There were only two biologists in high positions, but they spoke out often and volubly.

Even if one could accept a physicist as chief of state,

they argued, it was absolutely insane to make the vice-president a mathematician, that is, a creature from a parent tribe, if nothing worse, with the result that the two principal executives were men living in a fanciful world of inert particles and numbers with no knowledge of humanity. It was no surprise, they said, if things had reached an impasse because most administrative officials, who were also physicists, allowed themselves to be swayed by the two executives. The biologist faction was getting behind-the-scenes support from like-minded Nobels, who complained that the kind of testing used to select candidates for the competition had advantaged physicists shamefully. Some even went so far as to recommend dissolving the current administration and running a new series of fairer examinations.

To combat this campaign, secretly orchestrated by Sir Alex Keene, O'Kearn responded vigorously, bringing his prestige and influence to bear in support of the administration, and especially Fawell, who was discouraged enough to consider resigning.

During a meeting in which Nobels were discussing that possibility, O'Kearn convinced them that to admit defeat would have a disastrous effect on world opinion. "Neither the choice of high officials nor the rank assigned to them is the outcome of a lottery drawing or sample balloting," he reminded them emphatically. "It is the result of a rigorous competition organized by us, the Nobels, a single body, and we were its impartial judges. We cannot now call them incompetent without gravely impairing our own prestige and, by extension, the prestige of Science, which we need more than ever today."

It was the plain truth, and most of his colleagues agreed. Recalling the triumphs of the early years, O'Kearn declared that the government and its chief executive were not to blame. Of course, he admitted, certain problems seemed not to have been anticipated.

"But," he continued, "I see no reason why these baffling and distressing cases should fall within the competence of biological scientists rather than physicists and mathematicians."

At that point Sir Alex Keene was heard to sneer, eliciting muffled protests from the Nobel physiologists. Undaunted, O'Kearn pressed on:

"I repeat, they are not within the competence of either one or the other. This is not a disease like cancer, gentlemen, which we know you performed miracles to eradicate. It is not a matter of microbes, or virus, or bacteria. It is, we all agree, a disease of the mind. And such diseases are the domain of psychology. We were wrong probably, we Nobels most of all, not to have assigned sufficient importance to the human mind's ability to adapt. Probably we should have tested for that in the first examination. Now it is too late for regrets. We must find a cure. The mind is ill; we must seek help from specialists of the mind, its healers, the psychologists and psychiatrists. This is not only possible but easy, without changing the government one bit and without discrediting ourselves, since we are fortunate enough to have an eminent authority on such matters right at hand."

He reminded them that Mrs. Han had ranked second in the final examination, on a par with Yranne. The latter had been Fawell's choice for vice-president and had proved his capacity to think and to organize. He deserved their thanks. But present conditions called for the psychologist to fill his office, with extended powers and responsibilities.

O'Kearn concluded with the hope that Fawell could be

prevailed upon discreetly to make that cabinet shift, actually a very minor one in keeping with rules of procedure established when cabinet offices were first filled.

The Nobels could not reject such a practical proposal. Fawell resolved to implement it after talking to Yranne and finding that he had no objection. For some time Fawell himself had been considering the idea of bringing Betty into closer collaboration. She accepted the vice-presidency.

"Do you think you can find a remedy for the present situation?" he asked her anxiously.

She said she hoped to, having given a good deal of thought to it, but only if they assured her a liberal budget and adequate staff. "Like all sciences," she reminded him, "psychology cannot function without reading rooms, laboratories, and numerous competent specialists."

"You shall have everything you want, I promise you," the President told her. She was their one salvation. "You have a free hand."

Betty Han's first act was to establish a new office under her direction as Vice-President. That was how the Department of Psychology came into being.

1

THE STADIUM held five hundred thousand spectators, all seats above a certain level provided with field glasses to afford a front-row view. Still, it came nowhere near to accommodating the vast games-starved public. In addition, the entire television industry was mobilized to insure worldwide coverage of the event. Citizens everywhere thus could view live the world championship super-wrestling-team finals to be held that evening.

In fact, virtually the whole human race was watching, those not among the privileged five hundred thousand having abandoned ordinary occupations and distractions to glue themselves to their sets well in advance of the start, desperately anxious not to miss a single breathtaking moment or, worse still, the finish if one team managed to win an early victory, which had happened once during the semifinals.

Mrs. Han had insisted on personally presiding over

the contest, and her entrance drew a warm response. Five hundred thousand spectators gave her a standing ovation the moment she appeared with several aides. Betty had become immensely popular, hailed universally as the woman who had banished dread melancholy, stemmed the first wave of suicides, and who, gradually and judiciously, relying on the bold innovations and intelligent guesswork of her staff, had succeeded in restoring self-confidence to those poor mortals dispossessed of it.

Many colleagues envied her and would not attend the finals. Fawell was not one of them, as he valued the effects of her work; but he had elected to stay away in order to let all the glory fall on the Vice-President. Yranne had come, bringing his friend Zarratoff, whom he managed to drag there despite the astronomer's extreme aversion to games.

Yranne had gone to see him that morning and found him in his usual attitude when not preoccupied by government affairs. Hunched over his desk, gazing at a map of the heavens spread out before him, Zarratoff adored speculating on the origin of planets and the nature of the Universe. Yranne was not put off by the indignant protests that greeted his invitation to attend the games.

"You ought to be ashamed, disturbing me for *that* when I'm working. I refuse to devote a single minute to such futile spectacles."

"It promises to be an interesting sight. You ought to see it at least once to know what you're condemning."

This argument finally convinced the astronomer, who allowed himself to be drawn into the stadium.

A number of Nobels had already arrived and seemed no less excited than the rest of the crowd waiting tensely for the opening of what promised to be an unforgettable performance.

Betty Han found her seat and stood in front of it, facing the band. The audience followed her example as the players struck up the international anthem, the definitive text of which everyone now knew by heart and that many spectators were singing.

The stadium, built in the form of a truncated cone, was actually an immense circus, its sandy arena forming a circular ring of unique dimensions, separated from the audience by a tall iron railing instead of the traditional ropes. The two teams and three referees were standing in the center of the ring. Each team included two men and two women, still in their dressing robes, motionless as they listened to the world anthem. Floodlighted banners celebrating the naked truth decked the stadium's circumference.

The music stopped. Whispers rising from the tiers died out when Mrs. Han began to speak.

"I decla[illegible] the world championship finals in mixed-team superwrestling formally open. I and my Department wish the contestants good luck. Go to it, and may the best team win."

She then gave the international salute recently introduced by the government, arms raised parallel above the head, symbol of Science forever reaching out to progress.

The eight wrestlers responded with the same salute. Betty took her seat; the audience followed. The tier lights went out; darkness enfolded the floodlit ring. A referee introduced the teams.

"On my right, the Alpha team, representing the quantum theory; on my left, the Betas, champions of neo-Darwinism."

Each team acknowledged the introduction with another salute as the crowd cheered. Individual athletes were then presented.

"On the Alpha team, Miss Lovely, a student of the physical sciences."

Male and female wrestlers were applauded each in turn, but the greatest ovation went to Miss Lovely, a fair creature barely twenty, who was popular on several accounts. During the elimination matches and the semi-finals, she had emerged as a formidable wrestler, marvelously lithe, agile, and intrepid. She certainly deserved the *nom de guerre* "Lovely," a public tribute which she had adopted professionally. She was graceful and pretty despite a mannish haircut; without a dressing gown, her superb figure contrasted sharply with the coarse and lumpier shapes of the other women contestants. These assets were all the more alluring because, like everyone on both teams, female as well as male, Miss Lovely wore nothing but a pair of abbreviated trunks.

The salvo of applause that greeted her dignified yet provocative disrobing — an unannounced striptease adding spice to the occasion — was directed as much to her athletic prowess as to her splendid breasts. The latter fairly thrust themselves at her audience as, with arms raised in another salute, she wheeled around several times catching every eye in the crowd.

"Combat in a single bout not to end until one team is annihilated," the referee announced.

At the sound of a gong, intense silence blanketed the stadium while the finalists geared themselves for combat, unsheathing the dagger each carried lodged in his waistband.

2

THE CONTEST opened on a novel note. Ordinarily, men were pitted against men in spectacles of this type, and women against women. Yet here was The Killer, a legend among wrestlers, a hairy colossus with gorillian torso, at grips with Miss Lovely, his monstrous hulk towering above her. He and his teammates had obviously planned the maneuver, which scores of jeering onlookers protested as foul play. Miss Lovely was the favorite by far over any female Beta, but her elimination at the start (for what chance did she stand against this 260-pound cave man?) would set the Alphas behind. Hoots and hisses filled the air until the head referee raised his hand for silence, shaking his head to indicate that no rule had been broken. Miss Lovely accepted the challenge with a smile and turned to face her adversary.

The rules of the game left wrestlers free to do whatever

they chose except leave the ring or employ a weapon other than their dagger, which had to be the regulation type approved by the Wrestling Commission. Apart from that, there were no holds barred and contestants could fight with fists and teeth, could gouge out eyes, strangle their opponents, and, of course, use their knives. The booing died away as all eyes focused anxiously on the ill-matched pair.

The Killer was eager to get the business over with as one of his women teammates had been forced to take on a male Alpha, the weakest of the lot but still more than a handful for her until the Killer himself could come to her aid after polishing off Miss Lovely.

With his left arm folded protectively over the region of his heart, dagger upraised, he lunged at the girl, who waited motionless, scrutinizing every muscle he moved. The first attack failed. Miss Lovely evaded the knife with a sensuous wriggle. Applause crackled when she suddenly whirled around, caught the wrestler off balance and drew the first blood. The tip of her blade grazed his shoulder. Neither well-aimed nor powerful, the blow was a mere pinprick to this gorilla, whose scarred limbs testified to the many others he had received. Still, as the scarlet patch on his shoulder broadened, the stamping mob grew wilder.

Besides height and strength, The Killer had excellent reflexes. He launched a second assault before the girl had had a chance to catch her breath. Just as she was turning to face him, all 260 pounds of the colossus came hurtling down on her, catapulted by one of those forward leaps traditional to the ancient sport and dear to the hearts of superwrestlers.

The impact appeared to stun her; staggering, she

dropped her weapon and collapsed in the sand. The crowd roared angrily to see the wrestler scramble to his feet and plunge at her again, brandishing his dagger.

The rest happened so fast that many spectators came away with the wrong impression. Later on, slow-motion television detailed this memorable episode so that everyone could marvel at Miss Lovely's courage and incomparable strategy. She had suffered far less than it seemed, and if she lay there on her back clutching a fistful of sand in her left hand, it was not to ease the pain, as her adversary and the crowd assumed. Finding her at his mercy, and anxious for the kill, the man grew careless. Just as he raised his arm, the fistful of sand she had scooped up hit him square in the face, blinding him. His fatal mistake was to fling both hands over his eyes, for at that moment the dagger she had dropped within reach as she fell plunged straight into the heart beneath that hairy chest.

He fell dead upon the girl's body, and before she had time to flip him off with a toss of her hips, her own chest was bathed in blood, leading some spectators to presume that she too was mortally wounded, whereupon a desolate, mournful silence invaded the stadium.

Only when she sprang to her feet, alert and triumphant, as her adversary's body contracted in one final spasm, did the crowd grasp the truth. The concrete stadium began to rock beneath a storm of applause and unearthly howls, proclaiming victory for the favorite, who instantly became their idol. Officials shared in the general euphoria; Mrs. Han, an expert in such matters, hailed the triumph of intelligence and cunning over brute force while five hundred thousand voices roared the name of Lovely. Attending Nobels — the physics faction at least — contributed to the din, ardently supporting the Alpha team representing the quantum theory. Flushed with pride over a victory they took for their own, the elated physicists were in a frenzy, thrashing their arms about, drumming their feet, slobbering, belching, yelling and screaming meaningless noises.

"How do you like it?" Yranne asked Zarratoff with a wry smile.

The astronomer had watched the fighting in silence, intensely absorbed like everyone else. His friend's question caught him just as he was about to applaud impulsively. He gave a start, looking sheepish, then dropped his hands and simply shrugged. He never answered the question.

The crowd concentrated now on the other contests, having been distracted by the dramatic star attraction. One of the combats, between a male Alpha and a female Beta, was about to end tragically. The woman had fought valiantly at first, but two knife wounds sealed her fate. Courage suddenly failed her as she saw her opponent poised for the kill. Exhausted and hopelessly outmatched, her eyes begged for mercy. Dropping to her knees in the wrestler's path and bowing her head, she folded her arms over her bloodstained breast.

Howling indignantly, the crowd proceeded to pelt the poor creature with projectiles hurled through the railing. She was breaking a rule of the game that specified a fight to the death. The audience settled down only after the referee intervened and, at pistol point, forced the woman to stand up. She staggered to her feet. Her adversary threw down his dagger and again the crowd howled with rage. The referee prepared to intercede a second time, having also misinterpreted the act. But instead of sparing his victim, the wrestler simply intended to finish her off barehanded. He knocked her to the ground with his fist, straddled her body, and promptly throttled her.

Reassured, the spectators burst into wild applause, for even if this match was artistically inferior to the previous one, they always appreciated a fighter whose style displayed some variety.

An Alpha victory seemed a foregone conclusion. Yet during this interval, one of the two remaining combats, between a pair of men, was turning out badly for the team. The Alpha wrestler was losing. Flat on his back, with one arm broken from a brutal lock, his only defense lay in trying to wriggle clear of blows. He managed to dodge several, but the next proved disastrous. The Beta wrestler's triumph soon faded, however. As he knelt beside his victim summoning energy to deal the *coup de grâce*, the crowd broke into cheers, thinking the man deserved it even if he was not a favorite, then suddenly fell silent, watching with rapt attention. Having disengaged herself from her first victim, Miss Lovely was now inching forward. After several moments of intense stillness, a new wave of roars hailed the flashing dagger that buried itself in the transient victor's back. The blade plunged so deep that it took all the girl's strength to withdraw it, with one knee wedged against the lifeless body, which rolled over onto the Alpha wrestler.

The spectacle was nearly over, or so most of the audience seemed to think, because if two unscathed Alphas now were free to aid their teammates, according to the rules, then the world championship was as good as decided and the remaining contest promised little diversion.

It matched two female wrestlers, who thus far had merely scratched each other. But when one of them, the

Beta, saw Miss Lovely and her victorious partner approaching, she panicked at the prospect of three partners falling upon her all at once and begged for mercy, unleashing a fresh storm of public scorn and abuse. Courage deserted her. Dropping her dagger, she ran for safety when there was none. She rushed to the edge of the ring and circled it, clawing the iron railing and, in desperation, shaking it violently. But the bars were solid, designed to prevent escape. Pike-wielding stadium guards patrolling the outer perimeter prodded the poor creature back toward the center, into the arms of her three adversaries. Motionless and wild-eyed, she waited there, not even glancing at the Alpha male wrestler and her recent female opponent who were preparing to attack from opposite sides.

Miss Lovely, who had not joined in this maneuver, suddenly shouted, "Leave her to me!"

Savoring the event in store, the crowd urged her on, screaming, "Yes! Yes! Lovely! Lovely!"

Everyone welcomed this new element of suspense. Those about to leave sat down again. The male and female Alpha wrestlers looked at each other hesitantly, for each individual victory earned a special premium and Miss Lovely had already accumulated more than her share.

"Lo-ve-ly! Lo-ve-ly! Lo-ve-ly!" the crowd roared.

"Leave her to me," the girl insisted. "Please leave her to me and you can have all the premiums."

Her partners nodded, smiling, no doubt attracted as much by the generous offer as by a desire not to disappoint the fans, and perhaps also beguiled by the roguish charm behind her plea.

They stepped back. The champion was in no danger. Although much heavier than Lovely, the Beta woman was hopelessly outclassed. She was winded besides, and too dazed to offer serious resistance.

Now it was Miss Lovely's turn to fling her dagger aside and confront her final opponent barehanded. The next few minutes provided a dazzling spectacle of classic wrestling that no one who saw it would ever forget, that at times attained its ancient sublimity, an enchantment to connoisseurs of the old school. Exhilarated, soaring to the pinnacle of her art astride the rapturous acclaim of five hundred thousand worshipers, the girl displayed the infinite diversity of her wrestling technique, her feline elasticity and energy, in a stunning performance that drew wilder and wilder roars.

It began with a hail of blows hammered out with grace and power, like flashes of lightning thrusting up out of her entire body. Beneath this avalanche, too dazed to anticipate where and when the next cuff would fall, the bewildered Beta could only think of burying her head in her arms as she reeled under fresh blows.

Seeing her thus, like a bull dazzled and maddened by swirling capes and banderillas, Miss Lovely proceeded to another exercise. Backing off several paces, she sprang again, launching that marvelously athletic physique like a missile. Her opponent went down as if hit by a battering ram, then picked herself up painfully only to have the goddess come sailing through the air and plant one flying foot in the pit of her stomach, the other square in her face. Five or six repeat performances followed, the Beta woman managing to drag herself to her feet a little more feebly each time, a little more shaken and dazed, only to be sent sprawling again.

Indefatigable Miss Lovely unleashed everything she had. A single concerted thrust of the muscles in that splendid nearly nude body, stained with her victims' blood, taut as a bow, sent her virtually soaring through the air. And having hit her target, she landed gracefully on her hands, pirouetted in the sand, and without stopping for breath swooped off again. Hers was an almost supernatural display of force and beauty that defied the laws of gravity. The crowd, the three referees and two surviving Alpha combatants gazed spellbound at her every movement, transfixed with awe. At that moment they worshiped Miss Lovely for bestowing this free gift on her admirers. Not a cheer was heard in that vast stadium, only the victim's panting, growing steadily wearier, and the faint, muffled swish of that flying body skimming the sand as it flitted around her.

Mounting excitement had reached such a pitch that the hushed stadium seemed about to explode. It was time to wind things up. Miss Lovely did so with the vigor of a great artist. When at last the woman lay stretched on the ground, knocked senseless, the girl bent down and took hold of her between the legs and under the chest; with a sharp thrust of her torso that accented her superb musculature, she swung aloft at arm's length a limp body seemingly twice as heavy as her own. Amid waves of applause, she whirled it around, like a public sacrifice — twice, three times, ten times — until the dance of rapturous triumph left her giddy. Then, dropping the inert body on the ground, she flipped it onto its stomach, and with one divine knee pressed firmly into its back, grabbed the neck and broke the cervical vertebrae.

One last spontaneous hush fell over the crowd as all ears strained to hear the bones cracking. After that, pandemonium. Seized by her two partners and borne triumphantly aloft, Miss Lovely stretched out her arms, arched her glowing body to a public gone berserk, incapable of bridling its passions, that rampaged through the stadium splintering seats, shattering field glasses, smashing everything in sight as it bellowed delirious tributes to its idol.

3

A FEW MONTHS earlier, Betty Han had obtained a desperate government's consent to enact the program she and a team of psychologists and psychiatrists had worked out to cure humanity of the ills threatening to destroy it.

The report she presented to the executive council included a detailed scientific analysis of the various afflictions requiring psychological treatment. In ordinary language, it boiled down to the following points:

The world was suffering from melancholy. Hence the number of suicides. Vastly increased leisure, an outgrowth of systematized labor, had not been properly organized in turn.

Education had failed to fill enough spare time or to satisfy the human craving for entertainment and distraction. Against Betty's advice, the Department of Leisure had restricted its games section to a beggarly budget, thus preventing it from accomplishing anything worthwhile. Quite the reverse, the highly popular international sporting events of former times had disappeared along with their host nations and nothing had replaced them. The sporting impulse, among the strongest human drives according to psychologists, had been flagrantly disregarded.

As for LCE, individual loss of self-confidence resulted from having transferred that confidence to infallible mechanical devices provided by science. The astronauts presented a classic case. During those long space journeys they grew so completely dependent on computers, which never made errors, that finally they could not lift a finger without prior instructions and approval from machines.

After developing and analyzing these points exhaustively, the report went on to suggest possible solutions, also based on fundamental assumptions.

To combat melancholy in this critical situation called for some kind of shock treatment designed to stimulate passionate interest. Entertainments would have to be devised, sensational enough (literally) to captivate men's minds during long stretches of idleness.

These distractions, which the Department of Psychology translated as games, should help to restore self-confidence in individual participants as well as spectators by stirring the imagination and senses in some striking way. Relentless logic led from there to the notion of brutal, violent contests demanding every ounce of energy from competitors.

The report then dealt with purely psychological questions, citing the countless experiments carried out in daily life or in the laboratory and stressing the function of aggression. Clever wording forced the reader to accept as logical and all but natural the idea of inaugurating a series of public spectacles in which competitors would fight to the death. As a test, they could start at once with a single pair of contestants, seasoned fencers, for example.

Experts predicted that the excitement generated by these duels would improve the situation rapidly but not enough to maintain permanent psychic well-being. Mrs. Han looked ahead still further and, before the games principle had even been adopted, her staff of specialists was at work extending and diversifying the program.

Having reached this conclusion, after being lulled for a while by the cunning enticements of logic, Fawell and his advisers backed off hastily and swore that they would never condone such barbarous practices. Still, being men of science, accustomed to thinking, they composed themselves and reflected, which left them decidedly confused. In this state of mind they appeared at the conference called by the President to discuss the project and hear arguments in its favor.

Fawell arrived at the meeting looking grim and weary. Because of the important decision awaiting them, the Nobels had sent a large body of delegates. Heading it was O'Kearn, who had persuaded the government to rely more heavily on psychology.

The debate was long and lively. Several officials proceeded to attack the plan in the name of morality and plain humanity. Mrs. Han listened calmly before responding. Playing on words, she commented that "humanity" was in the process of disappearing forever; and as she was addressing rational minds, she had no difficulty convincing them that a few deaths meant nothing compared to wholesale suicidal slaughter. As a matter of fact, she saw this as a profoundly humane remedy if it succeeded in stemming the fatal epidemic, as psychology experts claimed it would. Conscientious scientists could not fail to be jolted by this argument, and the debate waned. Zaratoff remained fiercely opposed, however, though not on moral or humane grounds. He rejected games *per se*, because they were childish; but no one paid much attention to his lone voice.

Turning to Fawell, Betty smilingly asked him if he had checked the latest suicide statistics. He acknowledged that the rate had risen beyond all predictions. A tragic silence fell upon the conference as it faced its responsibilities.

"Even if we decided to try this experiment, we would still have to find volunteers for the games."

Betty reassured him, staking her professional reputation on the certainty of getting all the volunteers they needed, and many more. They would have to turn some away and set up standards for selecting qualified applicants. In addition to the material rewards reserved for survivors (even in a world of guaranteed prosperity it is always possible to invent new ways to compensate merit, as for instance with works of art, which indeed are priceless), the mere prospect of a public triumph with maximum publicity and media coverage would entice a mob of amateurs. Even the likelihood of a glorious death before thousands of spectators would attract those tired of living, who would prefer it to a lonely, miserable death at the end of a rope or in some murky river.

"Among other ills, the world is suffering from a lack of celebrities," Betty declared, "and one of our aims is to produce some. I advised you once to adopt a world anthem and a world banner. Experience has proved me right. Today I tell you that a world state must have world celebrities."

A handful of officials remained unconvinced. O'Kearn

placed the full weight of his authority squarely behind Betty Han, declaring, "We are realists. We cannot turn down a realistic solution. I recommend that we make the experiment."

The word "experiment" proved an irresistible lure to this congregation of scientists. The government unanimously — except for Zarratoff's lone dissenting voice — decided to proceed with it.

Shortly afterwards the games began. At first they were ordinary contests between pairs of swordsmen. As the rules of fencing did not apply, they could move about, run, or leap as they chose, even use their fists if they had a chance. The resulting clashes were not unlike old-time cloak-and-rapier films except that the blades were not blunted, the wounds were real, and the contest ended only when one of the pair fell dead.

The first few matches were highly successful. The crowd thrilled to each phase of the struggle and, as Betty had hoped, the victors became world celebrities. Two weeks after the start of these spectacles, which took place in various parts of the globe and were broadcast by all the media, the suicide rate had declined by twenty-five percent. Fawell had to admit once again that the psychologist was right. He did it gracefully and gave Betty Han full authority to enact and perfect her program.

Knowing that the public ultimately would tire of duels, she kept her staff working at fever pitch. Teams of laboratory researchers worked round the clock to develop a wider range of rousing, absorbing games to sustain and further stimulate the enthusiasm generated by the first experiments. Thus superwrestling with mixed teams had been discovered. The world championship had enjoyed enormous success, the preliminary matches having been played all over the globe. The finale surpassed even the wildest hopes.

Oddly enough, the wrestling idea was the brainchild not of a professional psychologist but of the mathematician Yranne. He had not felt the least bit offended by Betty Han's promotion and, as a matter of fact, was glad to be rid of some responsibilities. Having carried a staggering work load in recent years, now he too found himself with time to spare. Instead of using it for independent analytical research, he indulged a curiously irresistible urge to reflect on the Chinese psychologist's program. It interested him and invited his logical, subtle intellect to devise new types of games, which infuriated his friend Zarratoff, who was deprived of a chess partner when Yranne retreated into thought.

One evening, somewhere in a chain of deductions that probably he himself could not have retraced, it occurred to Yranne that wrestling carried to its utmost limit, namely death, might turn out to be the ideal stimulus for arousing mass enthusiasm. He told Betty about it in a joking way to mask his timidity.

Instead of laughing as he had expected, she remained serious and thoughtful. Thanking him warmly, she took this new idea straight to one of her laboratories where it was examined, dissected, analyzed, and refined to the point of producing the current choice spectacle. The crowning touch came from a young and inexperienced psychology student named Rousseau, whom she had hired for her research staff because he seemed imaginative and because she felt that young people were singularly well adapted to this kind of work. It was his proposal to add women to the teams and have them fight in the nude, or virtually so, like the men, thus combining spicy sex with pungent violence. Mrs. Han complimented him for this novel idea and predicted a brilliant future for the young man.

The suggestion of naming opposing teams after various scientific theories was Betty's. She meant to revive the element of passion injected once upon a time when rival nations competed with one another. Fawell approved this wholeheartedly, hoping to rouse an interest indirectly, through the games, for these theories, which would benefit Science in the long run.

As it turned out, though the rules had nothing to say on this score, the Alpha team almost always represented a physics doctrine and the Betas fought under the banner of some cherished biological principle.

4

AFTER THE world championship, the Department of Psychology appeared to be resting on its laurels and invented no new games for quite a long time. Research went on all the same, but none of the plans submitted to Mrs. Han satisfied her. She felt, surely for good reasons, that super-wrestling was something of a masterpiece next to which any other novelty would seem pale.

There were a few interesting ones, however, which she studied attentively: a type of rugby in which players wore spiked helmets; a cavalry charge with two teams armed with the metal-tipped lances of ancient tournament days rushing at each other at full tilt. Another plan, borrowed from the Roman amphitheater, featured paired combats between *retiarii* [unarmored fighters with net and trident — Trans.] and *mirmillos* [heavily armored gladiators — Trans.] or gladiators pitted against wild beasts.

She simply filed these plans away in case of need, hoping her staff would come up with better ones. For the present, superwrestling fulfilled human desires. The suicide rate was declining steadily, approaching normal. President Fawell began to take heart. It would be time enough to press for another creative effort when the current fad lost its popularity. That day would come, Betty was certain, but she wished it would take its time.

Meanwhile, the spectacular pyrotechnics ignited by the world championship had not died out. On the contrary, it blazed away for several months, fueled by the memory of that marvelous finale when Miss Lovely revealed herself in all her glory. She was now venerated like a goddess, a status never attained by the celebrities of yesteryear. All the media chanted daily odes to her incomparable talent and beauty. Her admirers numbered in the billions, and ghastly crimes were committed for the sole purpose of attracting her attention. Mrs. Han and her psychologist aides considered this agitation salutary and, behind a barrage of publicity, did everything they could to sustain the mood of feverish excitement which was dissipating last year's horrendous melancholy. Statistics backed them up. Miss Lovely was indeed a potent therapeutic agent; Fawell knew it and insisted on further glorifying her by personally pinning the world medal of honor upon her valiant breast.

After savoring their triumph for several months, the world champions were obliged to defend their title when challenged by a team of newcomers who had been training secretly. This time they were beaten. All four had their throats cut, and Miss Lovely's blood also flowed onto the sandy arena while her victorious rival, an even younger girl, screamed exultantly and danced upon the corpse. The world wept and groaned, but several days later, much to the Psychology Department's relief, the rival became an idol, stirring the howling mob to even wilder and noisier follies. Rousseau, the promising young member of Mrs. Han's research staff who had helped develop the superwrestling program, smilingly commented to her one day that celebrities of this order were not likely to wear out and end up miserable and forgotten because occupational hazards more or less limited their survival to a few months. In this manner the public's passionate interest was constantly restored and refreshed.

The psychological campaign scored another success: LCE, or loss of confidence in the ego, after receding drastically along with the wave of suicides, was about to fade into memory. Patients had only to attend one or two superwrestling matches to regain their self-confidence miraculously. For some, merely seeing the event on a television screen produced a noticeable improvement.

Not for everyone, however. Some cases defied the cure, including a number of astronauts, the first victims and probably the most severely afflicted. Nicholas Zarratoff was among them: his condition had not altered and he still suffered frightful attacks of LCE at fairly close intervals. After dragging him to several spectacles, some very fine indeed, Ruth noted despairingly that Nicholas had made no visible progress, and he realized it also.

When medicine and psychiatry proved helpless, Fawell and Zarratoff, Sr., grief-stricken and expecting the marriage to fall apart, decided to ask Betty's advice. Fawell now looked to her as to Providence in desperate situations, and the astronomer, after having become so absorbed in the championship finals, was almost prepared to forgive her for popularizing games.

The Chinese psychologist narrowed her eyes as she always did in moments of intense reflection. "I see only one remedy," she announced at last, "but I cannot reveal it either to you or to Ruth. I promise to speak to Nicholas privately."

That was all she would say, but she kept her word and talked to the astronaut in one of his lucid moments, telling him that she thought his only hope of recovery was to participate in one of the games, not as spectator but as competitor.

Nicholas was athletic and had once played a number of sports. He allowed himself to be persuaded, trained secretly for a month, then competed in an encounter, unknown to his wife or close friends. He felt that the psychologist was right. It was his last hope, the one chance to regain his sanity and escape what had become an unbearable torment, threatening to drive him down the beaten path to suicide.

He was fortunate enough to win and to stab two opponents with his own hands, a man and a woman, in a bout that drew cheers. The experience transformed him; after a series of examinations, the doctors pronounced him perfectly normal. He had no more difficulty operating a car or plane and was considered fit once again for space missions. The day he told Ruth about his therapy and complete recovery she wept and hugged him, made him swear never to do it again, and with a grateful heart, went off to lay exotic blossoms on the graves of his victims.

A number of astronauts who shared his indifference to spectacles followed his example and entered the games.

All of them were either cured or killed after the first session. LCE thus vanished forever from our planet.

As for the third dilemma plaguing the government, the leisure-laden public's lack of interest in pure science, it was hard to see that the Department of Psychology had made progress there, as Betty sometimes claimed. Any improvement in that area seemed to affect only the men of science. Now that public demand for new products had leveled off, scientists were no longer under constant pressure to produce them and could break free of the industrial technology colossus in order to resume basic research. Once again they could devote themselves to the objective pursuit of truth and the advancement of Science, which more or less had ground to a halt since the advent of world government.

It was not what Fawell had dreamed of. In fact he had the impression that civilization was heading straight for that division into two classes of individuals he had so dreaded once, and which now perhaps he would be forced to accept as a lesser evil. In moments of depression he often repeated to himself the words of Teilhard that had inspired his founding program:

> . . . The moment will come — it is bound to — when Man will admit that Science is not an accessory occupation for him but an essential activity, a natural derivative of the overspill of energy constantly liberated by the Machine.

For the present, the derivative was artificial and took the form of savagely inhuman games. In his talks with Betty, she would admit this openly, yet claim that it had achieved a first step. In a sense, public interest in science was awakening through the agency of competing teams representing themselves as champions of this or that theory. Words like "atom," "molecule," and "cell" were commonly used now because of the games. In time she hoped — and this was the aim of all her thinking, her grand design — to transfer this passion for the symbolic representatives of an idea to the idea itself. It would be a truly remarkable climax, one had to admit, a triumph of psychology crowning the miraculous results already obtained with superwrestling.

5

THE DAY FORECAST by Mrs. Han finally arrived when superwrestling no longer satisfied mankind's ravenous appetite for excitement; indeed the public was beginning to weary of it.

One morning Fawell called at the psychologist's home to discuss a highly confidential matter he did not want leaked. Wasting no time, he thrust at her a graph of the suicide rate, the real one, which a special bureau delivered to him personally every day. Barely glancing at it, Betty shrugged her shoulders.

"I know," she said. "Don't you think I have my own statistics? And everything bears them out. The latest games were disappointing. Even without my applause meters registering the precise reaction to every spectacle, I could have guessed it from the faces in the crowd."

"Melancholy?" Fawell asked grimly.

"Not overt, but surely impending."

No general display of that dread sullenness was yet in evidence. Spectators cheered, even shouted occasionally if the wrestlers happened to be outstanding or if some frail creature managed to polish off a brutish assailant, as Miss Lovely had done; but for sensitive observers like the psychologist, the applause had a different ring. It lacked any spark of enthusiasm. The wrestlers felt this too, and it affected their performance. Like an actor beginning to suspect mere politeness behind the applause and whose acting suffers accordingly, a wrestler rarely was able to achieve the peak of his art. One of them even behaved in the oddest fashion: Dejected, stretched out on the ground though not seriously hurt, he refused to get up and, without lifting a finger in his own defense, calmly waited for the referee to put a bullet in his neck. All this because public apathy had demoralized him.

These were alarming symptoms, and the suicide curve, which Fawell held out for Betty's inspection, confirmed the crisis in geometric language. From an extended plateau it was now tending to climb; barely perceptible as yet, just a slight rise, but Yranne, who studied it daily at the President's request, predicted a new upward surge. No expert in analytical geometry could mistake the signs.

"Appalling," murmured Fawell.

"I'm aware of that."

"We've *got* to do something."

"Don't you think I know it? I have a hundred specialists working right now in my laboratories. Believe me, I don't allow them a moment's peace; they realize how desperate the situation is. They've been racking their brains night and day to devise some thrilling, captivating game to replace superwrestling, which is now inadequate and on its way out."

"So?"

"So?" she repeated with raging impatience. "So they haven't come up with the right answer. They will eventually, I'm certain, but when?"

"A matter of days, maybe hours," Fawell said gloomily. . . . "Do you think we ought to try your cavalry charge?"

Once she had told him about the plans filed away for an emergency.

"Maybe so," she answered without conviction.

They gave it a try. With advice from the Department of Psychology, the government made elaborate arrangements for presenting this new game.

Each team was to have fifty riders (the psychologists felt the spectacle's drama would increase in direct proportion to the number of participants), twenty-five men and twenty-five women, a tried and proven ratio; armed with lances, they would charge full tilt against one another. Survivors of the onslaught had to occupy the enemy position, wait for a signal, then charge again, over and over until one of the teams was totally obliterated.

This called for large numbers of participants and promised to end in consistent wholesale slaughter. They would need to provide a steady supply of riders. But as Betty had also predicted, they had more volunteers than they needed of both sexes. To assure high standards of competition, the recruits were given intensive instruction in handling the lance and in horsemanship. An army of horses would be needed as well, which posed a problem because the scientific society had a shortage of the animals.

The government did not scrimp. It was prepared to

make sacrifices to conjure the demon Melancholy whose specter now haunted the earth again. It built training grounds and stud farms to develop an equine breed suited to this particular use. It designed special athletic fields, the ordinary arena being far too narrow. To augment the difficulties and the challenge, it decided to hold the jousts in open country pitted with all sorts of obstacles like streams and forests, and to have the riders dash several hundred yards before colliding. It searched out and located a number of appropriate sites, taking care to build public facilities which would not damage the terrain's natural assets. This was the reason for constructing two parallel sets of tiered seats and having the clash take place in between.

The whole elaborate project was carried out admirably, and the first tournament proved fairly successful. Riders took their appointed places in front of a curious crowd. The impact was rather impressive as tightly packed ranks of men, women, and horses produced a ghastly carnage. The action was so furious that only three or four riders on each side were left after the fourth interval. The desired result came after the sixth, when one team had been wiped out and only two victors survived.

The crowd cheered the new heroes lustily and applause meters registered an acceptable din. Fawell suddenly took hope as the suicide rate dipped, but Betty Han shook her head skeptically. Doubt and professional experience warned her that the situation would not last.

She was right. Subsequent tournaments met a lukewarm response, and very soon it became apparent that cavalry charges were just a passing fad. To meet the critical need for new games, they tested several of the emergency projects. Gladiatorial combats proved unpopular and lasted only two weeks. Rugby with spiked helmets turned into a fiasco played out in gloomy silence, generating only diffident, sporadic applause from the fourteen-and-under sector. The demon Melancholy refused to be exorcised by such entertainments, and its reeking specter once more darkened the sky.

6

THE SUICIDE rate had been climbing for a month. Hard as she pressed her staff of experts and was hounded in turn by a frantic Fawell, no one could invent a game exciting enough to halt the fatal epidemic.

The Vice-President felt despondent that morning as she entered one of the psychological research laboratories to examine a new project reported by her chief of staff. Valuing Yranne's judgment, she had asked him to come along. Had he not devised *the* game of the age? Besides, he was as interested as ever in the work of her department and found himself spending more and more spare time trying to imagine remedies for the present sad state of affairs. Betty often begged him for help.

"Can't you come up with another idea like superwrestling?"

But he too seemed to be suffering from mental torpor and had nothing acceptable to offer.

The laboratory chief sat them both at his desk and gave Betty the file covering the new invention. She and Yranne studied it.

The project seemed original enough but struck Betty, even before she had examined it in detail, as just another weak palliative. It consisted of an underwater combat between frogmen and frogwomen carrying guns like those once used in undersea fishing but with greater range and accuracy, as well as knives to pierce chests or an opponent's oxygen line in hand-to-hand fighting. The game was planned for a giant glass-faced aquarium ringed with seats.

"What do you think?" Betty asked her companion.

Yranne grimaced and did not answer immediately. All around, researchers were working silently, nearly fifty of them in this one laboratory, all young, many still earning degrees or just lately in receipt of one. The psychologist continued to rely on youthful imagination to discover a miracle cure. Individual worktables and drawing boards encouraged them to study and elaborate the visual aspects of new plans. Occasionally, if a proposal seemed promising, they could have a professional draftsman render it in color.

In a studio adjoining the laboratory were facilities for testing the effects produced by volunteer actors on spectators chosen more or less at random. Cameras and a projection room made it possible to analyze every sequence of a game with an eye to eliminating the tiresome ones and retaining only the thrills.

These budding scientists were free to do whatever they wished and were judged solely on the results. Their working habits varied: Some chose the group approach, discussing ideas with their colleagues and collaborating with them; others preferred independent research and presenting only finished pieces of work.

Noting Yranne's mute, unenthusiastic response, Betty turned to the laboratory chief standing on the far side of the desk.

"And what do *you* think, Rousseau?"

He was the same student who had attracted the attention of psychology experts. Betty had put him in charge of the laboratory, hoping the promotion would stimulate his inventiveness. On that point she seemed to have erred, for it had the opposite effect of animating his critical faculties and dulling the creative ones.

"It has interesting aspects, Mrs. Han," he replied, "otherwise I wouldn't have asked to show it to you."

His hesitant tone seemed to belie his words.

"Explain yourself," she pressed him impatiently. "It sounds as if you're holding something back. Don't hesitate to criticize; that's what I'm here for."

"It's this way, Mrs. Han —"

"I have a criticism," Yranne cut in abruptly. "A small matter which the inventors and you yourself, Rousseau, appear to have overlooked. . . . Too much blood, Betty, too much blood."

Pursing her lips, Betty threw up her hands in exasperation. "Really, Yranne, I assumed this one drawback of all our games had been reduced once and for all to its proper perspective. Are you joining up with the people who call us butchers when, in fact, we are saving thousands of lives? You know well enough that to arouse passion you must first spill a little blood. I didn't expect such a remark from you, Yranne," she said, looking utterly dejected.

"Relax, Betty. You don't see what I was driving at."

"I think I can explain what you meant, Mr. Yranne," Rousseau interrupted boldly, "and also prove that I didn't overlook this objection. Actually, it's contained in a separate note I added to the file which you haven't seen yet."

"Then read it to us."

Rousseau read: "One of the probable drawbacks of this type of combat is that the water is likely to become too murky after a few chests have been pierced, which may even prevent the audience from seeing the end of the spectacle."

"Congratulations!" shouted Yranne. "That's exactly what I was thinking."

"I must confess the point escaped me," Betty murmured.

"It also seems to have escaped the plan's designers," Rousseau observed somewhat disdainfully.

Mrs. Han eyed them both with keen interest and admiration, a combination rare for her. "You don't miss a thing, you two."

The young man grinned modestly. "It's just possible, as I also noted, that we can find a chemical process for eliminating the problem. We'll look into it."

"All right now. The first objection is too much blood," Betty said. "Are there any others?"

"There's at least one other which I think is even more important," Rousseau declared with a trace of mystery.

"What's that?"

"First, Mrs. Han, let me show you a test run we filmed. The defect sticks out like a sore thumb."

"You've tested it already?"

"In a fairly large outdoor aquarium I had them build. But in order to spare the staff I didn't finish the experiment. The projectiles are harmless, plain rubber darts. To make it more realistic, though, each jab releases a corresponding trickle of blood from a waterproof pocket, so we can watch the water gradually clouding up. But I think you'll be struck mainly by the serious defect I mentioned."

"We'll see. Experience is the best teacher."

Just before entering the projection room Betty stopped and turned to Rousseau, whose behavior seemed decidedly enigmatic.

"Rousseau, you're hiding something. You present me with a project that definitely holds together yet, according to you, has at least one serious drawback. I want an honest answer. Do you or don't you consider it valid?"

"I don't," he replied instantly.

"That's what I surmised. Yet for a project you reject *a priori*, you went to the trouble of testing it and recruiting actors, though you didn't allow them to be exterminated."

"I didn't because my demonstration didn't require it," Rousseau explained apologetically.

"I'm not holding it against you. . . . So according to what you've told me, for this demonstration you built a giant aquarium and made a film. Mind, I'm not blaming you for the expense either. I've always said, and I say it again, that whatever funds are needed for your research I will get, provided the research is fruitful. Now this particular experiment . . ."

"On my honor, Mrs. Han," Rousseau pleaded earnestly, "I found this experiment extremely useful and am certain it will prove fruitful despite the negative aspects."

Seeing that it was impossible to get anything further out of him for the moment, she gave a shrug and entered the projection room.

7

Betty sat down next to Yranne while Rousseau went over to give instructions to the projectionists. The lights dimmed as the film began. The opening sequences pleased the two executives. Like everything else this laboratory did, the test had been carefully conducted.

The visual impression was good. Expert lighting cast fantastic quivering reflections around the swimmers, men and women chosen for their admirable physiques and aquatic skill, who seemed to move about in a supernatural universe devoid of gravity. They chased each other tirelessly, one trying to corner an opponent for a direct hit, while the latter, diving in a swirl of spray, slithered eel-like between his legs and struck him in the back. When jabbed by a dart, one swimmer brilliantly enacted his own death throes, which took on new, unexpected drama in those watery depths, the simulated spurts of blood depositing throbbing patches of color, like scarlet jellyfish, throughout the iridescent aquarium.

"Not bad at all," Yranne whispered.

Betty did not answer. One minute she was tempted to agree, only to find herself feeling extremely uncomfortable an instant later, burdened by a vague sense of oppression. It had nothing to do with the fact that a few mock stabbings had turned the water cloudy, obscuring the end of the struggle. That was a purely physical detail, which, as Rousseau had pointed out, could be rectified. No, it was something else, a defect she felt intuitively was glaring, though it persistently eluded her. Yranne seemed to share this impression as he remained silent for the remainder of the film, which ended a quarter of an hour later.

"What do you think, Mrs. Han?"

Betty's nerves were so taut that the unexpected question pronounced in an abnormally loud voice right next to her ear made her jump. Yranne reacted the same way. After the lights came on, both of them sat silent and motionless, as if hypnotized.

Proud of her self-possession, Mrs. Han hated to be caught in a rare bout of nervousness. She turned angrily on Rousseau, who had moved up noiselessly behind her seat toward the end of the film and was responsible for the untimely outburst.

"There's no point trying to startle me that way," she complained irritably.

"I beg your pardon, Mrs. Han," he answered contritely, "but . . . I did it on purpose."

"What?"

"I did it on purpose," he repeated firmly. "It's an extension of my experiment."

Yranne began to examine him with new interest.

Adopting a humbler tone, Rousseau confessed, "It's a simple little psychological test."

"And I suppose we've served as guinea pigs," said Betty, more puzzled now than angry. "But I don't see —"

"I surprised you simply to dramatize the impact of this game on your state of mind. Your reaction proves that it depressed rather than elated you."

"You may be right. But what caused the depression?"

Lowering his voice mysteriously, Rousseau replied, "Haven't you felt it, Mrs. Han? The world of silence."

"What about the world of silence?" Betty countered in annoyance.

"The fellow's a genius!" exclaimed Yranne. "I know just what he's driving at, Betty."

"Good for you."

"The experiment proved extremely valuable, Mrs. Han, by disclosing, even accentuating, a major failing common to all our games. The absence of —"

"Of sound!" Yranne bellowed. "Just as I thought. No noise! He's a genius, Betty!"

"No noi . . ." In a flash she understood. For some time now she had had a nagging feeling that previous failures could be traced to some very simple yet elusive cause. "I see; yes, I see," she murmured, "but go on with what you were saying."

Rousseau's chest billowed out. "Well, Mrs. Han, even if I don't have a plan of my own to submit yet, I think I've discovered the defect in all our previous inventions, including superwrestling. Take the latter for example: the visual impact was excellent, perfect, and that's why it lasted so long; but its auditory effect was nil; it had no sound, no noise. One can only captivate human beings by appealing to all their senses, at least the principal ones."

"He's right," Yranne exclaimed. "We've been fools."

"And I the biggest one," Betty complained bitterly. "How could I ignore the auditory element when I was the one to promote the fireworks and the universal hymn? How could we be so blind?"

"Deaf is probably what you mean," Rousseau corrected, grinning. "If you don't mind the comparison, I'd say our games resemble the old silent screen. It produced a few masterpieces, but people finally tired of it and wanted sound. Sound isn't too important at first, in wrestling, for instance, when the visual element is stimulating; the crowd feels compensated by its own cheers and shouts. But that isn't enough in the long run. Our cavalry charges brought galloping hoofbeats and crashing lances, not nearly a fitting accompaniment. Arousing mass enthusiasm calls for a much broader range of sounds. As for these underwater games unfolding in dead silence, they are bound to fail, and today's demonstration was only intended to focus on this perpetual stumbling block."

"A stroke of genius," Yranne murmured.

Betty Han, her self-possession restored, did not mistake the importance of Rousseau's remarks but chose to restrain her admiration. "Perhaps," she sighed. "Still, all this is negative. Don't you have something positive to propose? It's extremely urgent."

Rousseau said he had nothing yet, but was hopeful now that his research had taken a new turn as a result of his discovery.

Betty made it a practice to let her researchers work in their own fashion. She dismissed Rousseau with a smile of encouragement. He returned to his desk, the object of envious glances from all the young psychologists hunched over their worktables and drawing boards. The two executives left the laboratory.

"We may have nothing positive yet, but I think we've taken a great step forward," Yranne murmured. "I'm going to think about it too, and tomorrow I'll talk to Zarratoff."

"Why Zarratoff? How can astronomy help us?"

"He has the soul of a poet, and poets can be imaginative."

"He's been dead set against games all along."

"He *was*," Yranne corrected her, smiling enigmatically.

1

A TELEVISION SCREEN lit up at the back of the amphitheater. It was gigantic, in keeping with the events about to be recorded, and covered nearly the entire wall. Busts of Einstein and several other luminaries had been removed to storage so as not to block the view. An attractive blonde appeared, smiling bewitchingly, and announced:

"Good evening to you, ladies and gentlemen. In just a few minutes globovision will bring you direct, in three-dimensional color, with odor of course, the fourth game of the history series. The teams have taken their places. Our top reporters and cameramen are on hand to bring you on-the-spot coverage from key points, so I hope you won't miss a single moment of the competition. Ladies and gentlemen, have yourselves good days, superb evenings, and exhilarating nights, for the broadcast will continue uninterrupted until the end of the match, and certainly [her smile expanded] we have no idea how long that will be."

She vanished as a clock filled the screen. It was five minutes before midnight, but the "12" had been replaced by the letter H. A thrill raced through the amphitheater, where government officials, a number of prominent personalities, and the full complement of Nobels breathlessly awaited the new game. Rousseau had been invited to join this privileged company as a reward for outstanding services.

Other giant screens had been installed all over the world as the new game was far too dangerous for live audiences. But television networks had made every effort to simulate a direct experience, with armies of scientists and technicians standing ready to help them. Indeed every expert had cooperated to produce a truly flawless spectacle, a masterpiece of realism.

Excellent color reproduction had existed for some time of course, but recent improvements made it rival, if not surpass, nature's own vibrant tones and vivid contrasts. A group of the ablest physicists spent hours in the laboratory evolving these effects. Fawell had started out as adviser to the project, only to end up actively heading it. He too was becoming addicted to games.

A new process had been developed for capturing faultless three-dimensional images. As for sound, the quality had improved to the point where a vast repertoire of distortion-free sound effects was available to enhance the action, from an insect's chirping or a dying man's last gasp to the worst earsplitting clamor. O'Kearn himself had abandoned his nuclear research to serve technology and help produce this acoustical work of art.

As all odors were transmitted with absolute fidelity along with larger-than-life images that had lost none of their sharpness, televiewers were about to witness reality itself, broadcast by tens of thousands of receivers scattered strategically all over the globe and relayed nonstop by a set of artificial satellites, the location of which had been mapped by the astronomer Zarratoff.

In spite of all this, large numbers of fans remained unimpressed by the level of realistic perfection, electing to observe the contest in the flesh. They were allowed to do so at their own risk.

The clock vanished from the screen just as the hour hand reached H. Now the time was flashed onto the lower right-hand corner of the screen every second. It was midnight, yet special technical devices made it possible to televise the landscape as if it were only dusk. The spectacle opened with a series of lingering panoramic views from different angles, without human figures.

The first scene was a seascape, calm with gently rolling surf. Several cameras filmed it from various distances starting far out at sea and gradually nearing the shore, while ocean smells invaded the amphitheater. A sandy, pebbly beach unfolded next, with massive ridges rising at intervals, looking for all the world like rocks to the inexperienced eye.

"The casemates," whispered Sir Alex Keene, with a knowing smile. "*They*'ll get a warm reception."

As the outlines of these mounds emerged more distinctly, they appeared far too regular to be natural. As it turned out, they were concrete bunkers, and a close-up showed protruding guns trained on the open sea. Another camera, sweeping the beach, picked out a thick barbed-wire entanglement reinforced here and there with steel piles. Several shots of this followed, giving viewers a clear impression of several miles of shoreline.

The camera made its way back to the open sea, now dotted with all kinds of boats, an armada filling the screen and progressing slowly coastward. Then it focused in turn on the turrets of a destroyer, a smaller warship, and cargo vessels of various sizes.

The first human figures finally appeared on the decks of several ships. They were members of the Alpha team representing the physical sciences. Packed into a compact unit on the decks, their silence in itself was rather solemn. The only sounds, faithfully reproduced, were the lapping of waves and the low hum of engines.

But now another sound intruded, gradually dissipating the relative quiet, growing louder as seconds flashed by in the corner of the screen.

"*Our* planes!" O'Kearn exclaimed, staring defiantly at Sir Alex Keene.

They were indeed planes drawing near, flying in the same shoreward direction. Soon they were over the fleet, then beyond it, while camera crews began filming the skies. The planes were of various types and arrived in several waves. After some overall views, one cameraman moved in close enough on a heavy bomber to expose the open bomb bay with its lethal cargo.

It was nearly half past twelve. Globovision turned from sea to shore, where the hum of ships' engines was becoming more audible and a bustle of activity could be seen. Orders rang out in the night; shadows scurried in and out of shelters. Suddenly, on the dot of half past midnight, a deafening uproar erupted on land, on sea, and in the air, setting the giant screen ablaze.

Never had the image of any *real* battle produced the gripping effects of this spectacle. During the *real* Normandy landing in 1944, a few sequences had managed to convey the violent fighting, but camera crews had had to film on the run with limited technical equipment and no organization comparable to the present one. They could not be everywhere at once to give overall impressions and simultaneously capture a flood of graphic details, as did the current crews. And taped reconstructions of an event were bound to lack the matchless emotional and visual impact of *live* action.

Here, the game's organizers had stationed experts at key points, which they could single out in advance, having planned them. Specifying the where and when of the first assault was one of the rules of the game. Apart from that, teams were fairly free to do as they pleased. Safety measures had been taken to protect television crews, and at all friction points film units had been tripled, quadrupled, increased even tenfold to insure that in the event of a direct hit, spectators would not be deprived of some gripping episode.

This professional zeal reaped its rewards. The laborious preparations were not wasted, for the spectacle promised to be an extraordinary achievement. The first bombardment convinced Yranne that they had a winner and, nudging Betty's shoulder, he held out a clenched fist with the thumb erect, signifying approval. The audio-visual impact was unbelievable; audiences would have had to be wooden to resist such thrills.

The screen was constantly lit now by exploding bombs, with cameras frequently tracking their downward path from the moment of release until the torrential blast of fire and steel. Viewers could also watch the maneuvers of Beta teammates, members of the biological clan, who were defending the coast. A few separate sequences conveyed the flurry of activity inside bunkers, the relentless shelling, the feverish pounding of antiaircraft guns, all sustained, all sublimated by a sound track finally worthy of them: the steady crackling of firearms periodically punctuated by the roar of heavy artillery, an exalting symphony further enlivened by the battle odor permeating the amphitheater.

The scene was no less gripping in the skies above the Normandy coast where a meshwork of blinding flashes streaked the darkness. Searchlights captured moving forms blacker than the night as they emerged from clouds, which then appeared like gleaming stars incrusted in the cone of light that refused to release them. Now and then one of those stars would tremble and vanish, only to reappear in the blackness below as a trail of glowing smoke. One of the cameramen usually managed to track a plunging plane until it crashed, briefly drowning out the rest of the din and lighting up the sky again.

Unearthly fairy tale of incomparable dramatic vigor, this live presentation of a mammoth ordeal of uncertain outcome between champions expert at their trade created a mood of tense, thrilling expectancy from which no one could escape. The specter of the demon Melancholy had been cast out. Mrs. Han herself indulged for just a fleeting instant in the universal excitement, a flicker of triumph animating her normally frigid gaze.

2

THE NEW GAME, with "The Landing" its theme, was simple. One team tried to invade the European continent; the other was supposed to hurl the invaders back into the sea. It was the fourth in an exhilarating series that had turned into an enduring success.

Historic games, the guiding motif proposed by the Department of Psychology, had been adopted on a trial basis by the government, something for which they could now be proud of themselves. If young Rousseau's pivotal remark stressing the need for sound effects to match the quality of images engendered these creations, he could not claim sole paternity. The latter derived from close cooperation with Yranne and the astronomer Zarratoff, who, as the mathematician had implied one day to Betty, was undergoing a rather remarkable metamorphosis. Not only had he ceased repudiating games; he was even tempted to contribute an occasional stone or two of his own to this monument of psychology.

In fact the opening game in the series was conceived by Yranne and Zarratoff as the result of a happy coincidence: the conjunction of two unrelated trains of thought. When Yranne, still pondering Rousseau's judicious observation, went in to see his friend he found him hunched over his desk in a familiar contemplative posture. This time, however, instead of pouring over an astronomical map, Zarratoff was engrossed in a large rectangular board with red and blue movable pieces representing two hostile naval forces. Without a word, he simply waved his hand imperiously to show that he was involved in a complex maneuver and did not want to be disturbed.

The mathematician was not in the least put out. Drawing a chair up to the far side of the desk, he sat down silently and began studying the board also, looking for the best series of moves.

At last Zarratoff condescended to speak. "It's blue's turn. Choose your color."

"I'll take red. Your move."

The two friends had recently discovered this ancient game and taken to it with surprising relish. It replaced chess, the intricate maneuvers of which bored them now that their thinking had taken a different turn.

The match continued in silence. Yranne, who usually won, watched his ships sink one after another until forced to concede, which he did like a true sportsman. At first wildly exultant, Zarratoff then seemed puzzled at his friend's unwonted bungling.

"Your second move dumped a present in my lap. You ought never to have left your aircraft carrier exposed. Elementary."

Yranne apologized for the blunder. "I have something else on my mind," he explained.

Then he told him about the curious episode in the psychology laboratory the day before and Rousseau's conclusions. The astronomer nodded his head in silent appreciation, and the two of them began pondering the matter afresh, staring fixedly at the board.

"Good Lord!" Zarratoff exclaimed.

"Why, of course!" cried Yranne.

No one will ever know which of these two minds first sparked the idea. In any event, the theme of the first historic game sprang to life at that instant, and with it a glimpse of the basic principle behind these entertainments. The two scientists needed few words to communicate their brainstorm and arrive jointly at a practical application of it. Yranne snatched up the phone to call the psychology laboratory. Mrs. Han was there, talking excitedly with Rousseau.

"Betty, we've found it, Zarratoff and I."

"You too? . . . What is it?"

"Trafalgar."

"Trafalgar? . . . Yes, surely, why not Trafalgar . . . ?"

No further explanation was needed. The discussion with Rousseau had so oriented Betty Han's thinking that the one word sufficed. She smiled, contented to have experimental proof now of the fecundity of her laboratory chief's observations.

"Hold on a second," she told Yranne, then turned to Rousseau. "They've come up with Trafalgar. What do you think of it? . . ." She handed him the receiver. "Here, tell him yourself what we were discussing."

A look of annoyance flickered across Rousseau's face. "Yes, sir . . . Trafalgar? Not a bad idea at all. Now I was thinking . . . I mean *we* were thinking, Mrs. Han and myself, of The Battle of the Marne."

"The Battle of the Marne," Yranne repeated, looking pointedly at Zarratoff. "Say, that's not bad either."

"Still," the astronomer interrupted, "a naval engagement —"

"We'll do both," Betty exclaimed, snatching back the receiver. "We're supposed to cooperate, not quarrel. My compliments to both of you. Now I see what's to be done. We'll produce both of them and many more besides. We have an inexhaustible gold mine."

The principle of historic games had been born; only the details and rules needed to be worked out. Basically, it involved choosing epic events from the past which offered supremely rich and provocative audio-visual attractions bound to arouse enthusiasm, perfecting this last aspect first through painstaking analysis, then selective synthesis, and ultimately unveiling them to the world in the form of games.

The finished product would bear no resemblance, of course, to any slavish recapitulation of historic truths such as a film might present, its sole novelty residing in the flesh and blood victims. Suspense had to be maintained at all costs down to the very last second. The event served merely as a *theme*. The outcome as well as any number of episodes might deviate from chronicled reality, depending on the performers' talent, their commander's skill, and various other factors known to decide victory or defeat.

Opposing teams would face each other on the original battlefield (for it soon became evident that only famous battles could provide the desired results). Each team had the same number of men and started out at essentially equal strength. These conditions were not always easy to meet and demanded detailed long-range planning.

The players, volunteers as always (more and more kept applying), posed no problem, but supplies and equipment were another matter. The first game, "Trafalgar," was simple enough, with the central administration handling the whole affair. At H-hour of the contest, each team was given command of an entire fleet ready for operations, comprising an equal number of ships (twenty-seven for both the "English" and the "French," thus correcting historic inequalities) as well as matching arms, ammunition, and equipment. But after this initial experiment convinced the authorities that the public was being deprived of considerable diversion, they switched to the following *modus operandi:*

Several months before the date of the spectacle, they issued a list of contestants and left them to manage their own affairs, to appoint leaders and classify personnel at will, and to equip themselves for battle, which meant producing their entire arsenal of weapons and supplies. Each side was allotted matching quantities of raw materials such as minerals, chemical products and the like, and was assigned an active industrial complex. Because of the crucial need for experts, each team had the right to secure a certain number of scientific and technical advisers to run its factories and turn out the best products in the shortest possible time, in keeping with the rules of the game.

Initially, the rules directed contestants to manufacture and use only matériel contemporaneous with the historical event. But as this restriction seemed a shade too harsh and likely to inhibit creativity, it was amended, after several experiments, to provide for modernization of matériel on condition that no process be employed involving a major invention of later date. This introduced a measure of flexibility into research and development while diminishing the risk of disputes that might try the competence of umpires. In addition, a long index of licit and illicit practices was issued. In "Waterloo," for example, the second game of the series, motor vehicles obviously were forbidden, but the manufacture of longer, stouter cannon was authorized if technicians could produce more highly resistant alloys. Similarly, there was no objection to combining standard ingredients of the period in order to obtain a more effective explosive.

Plainly then, some of the games required extensive preparations, yet these in turn were engrossing enough to compensate for the unavoidable delay in presenting the spectacles themselves and served to boost public morale in between productions.

The lengthy prelude had become a game in itself, a game of patience, skill, and ingenuity; without inducing the driving passion of competition, it managed all the same to keep the public in suspense, with occasional flurries of excitement verging on exhilaration. And though part of this spadework was carried out behind the scenes, the sheer numbers of participants made secrecy impossible. Humanity had its own sources of information, ever on the lookout for the endless indiscretions and rumors of espionage reported in the press or implied by the summary execution of some secret agent. In fact once the teams were designated, they proceeded immediately to establish intelligence networks.

Of course the public also hungered to know whether

a contest would end as history recorded or in reverse, with the vanquished becoming the victor. As information trickled in, wagers mushroomed to the point where a last-minute report could make or break fortunes. These auxiliary diversions did more than their share to maintain a wholesome state of nervous tension throughout the world in the wake of banished melancholy.

People also reveled in rebaptizing team leaders. History had been confirmed more or less by the outcome of "Trafalgar," in which the Alphas triumphed under "Nelson," sinking the Beta fleet lock, stock, and barrel and drowning or slaughtering every last sailor. The victorious admiral survived, however, and became a popular idol — to his great relief, having nursed a superstitious lump in his throat throughout the game.

"Waterloo," on the other hand, handed victory to "Napoleon" after "Blücher" had been misled by false reports and "Grouchy" came to the rescue in time. But in "The Battle of the Marne" the "German army" prevailed on the heels of another splendid job of spying and sabotage. "Gallieni" attempted unimaginatively to revive the taxi escapade. (This attitude was not unusual and never failed to excite curiosity as to how far certain leaders would go in repeating tried and proven tactics.) But having learned the facts from its spies on the eve of D-day, the enemy managed to pour sugar into the fuel tanks of all Parisian taxicabs, which were easily recognizable. When the command to move was given, not one of them could budge.

The episode, especially this last sequence, was a triumph for globovision. Viewers roared with laughter at the wretched drivers moaning and cursing as they dismantled their engines but still couldn't locate the trouble. A commentator had just explained the situation in order to inform audiences about certain undercover activities that could not be televised. As presented, the scene recalled the finest achievements of the old hidden camera technique and won instant acclaim.

3

PREPARATIONS FOR a game demanded more time, effort, and facilities if the historic event was of more recent date. "Waterloo" took only four months to produce. Arms manufacture had been easy enough; the really delicate problem was finding and training enough horses, but the experience gained in staging those plain cavalry charges simplified the task. "The Battle of the Marne," calling for greater technical virtuosity, took six whole months to prepare.

A gestation period of one year was scheduled for "The Landing," rather short considering the vast organization required. An ulterior motive of Fawell's had prompted his insistence on that close a deadline. It occurred to him that the time element offered a thrilling challenge to the scientific skills and resourcefulness of the teams, for science, by the very force of circumstances, was taking an increasingly active part in these productions. In fact "The

Landing" gave scientists their first starring role in the games.

Suddenly the men of science found themselves in great demand. Knowing that defeat was inevitable without their expert guidance, that team leaders themselves were incapable of re-inventing gunpowder or tempered steel, these leaders eagerly sought to secure (as was their privilege) the services of eminent scientists and technicians. Once again the former had to suspend basic research programs. That was nothing new, whereas their manifest reluctance to protest it came as something of a surprise. Plainly flattered by the sudden attention, like ardent, exuberant teenagers, they knocked themselves out to repay it.

An extremely curious world phenomenon had appeared, which even Betty Han's subtle insight had failed to anticipate. In effect, the public had been drawn toward a certain form of science, applied rather than pure, which, if not precisely "sublimation of interest," at least represented an improvement. Offsetting this, however, was the fact that scientific thinking had undergone a matching deterioration, implying that both science and the public would wind up shortly at the same rather mediocre intellectual level.

The change affecting first Yranne then Zarratoff, a sudden craze for childish amusements, was not an isolated happening. Fawell himself had capitulated to it as well as O'Kearn. Others followed. It was an alarming but very real paradox that the men of science now stooped to share the concerns, the desires, and the joys of ordinary humanity. They were passionately interested in working for the games within the bounds prescribed, in other words, using the imperfect theories and techniques of earlier times. Sometimes they took childish delight in devising ingenious gadgets, pledging their honor *not* to avail themselves of previous scientific knowledge. Such as the nuclear physicist who had discovered how to release gigantic stores of energy from a tiny mass and now was indulging his puerile fancies in juggling the ingredients of this or that official gunpowder formula in order to arrive at maximum efficiency. For "Trafalgar," a wave specialist developed a visual communications system based on semaphores. Another great scientist tried to imitate Archimedes by setting fire to the enemy fleet, using mirrors. He managed to destroy only one vessel, but it was a highlight of the televised production and an unforgettable personal triumph.

In any event, pure science had not faded altogether from memory. Rival teams continued to symbolize some major branch of either physics or biology. This traditional pattern became plainer than ever in "The Landing," with Alphas standing for Physics unadorned, Betas for Biology.

Thus far the Alphas had won every time. In fact their opponents were clearly handicapped in arms production as all the arms specialists were physicists, who, not surprisingly, were serving their clansmen. The other side had had to digest the laws of inert matter at a furious rate in order to translate this into guns, shells, and explosives; the fact that their scholarly endeavors had failed so far to pay off enraged them. They were reported to be making superhuman efforts for "The Landing" in hopes of taking their revenge. Not only were they advantaged in possessing newly discovered antibiotics to treat the wounded, but were also rumored to have other unpleasant surprises in store for the Alphas.

Nobels were no less thrilled by the games. In principle,

neither they nor government officials could take part in the preparations, but most of them resolved to see their clan win and many ran the risk of giving clandestine counsel to secret agents approaching them under cover of darkness.

As for the pure mathematicians, they had proved remarkably adept at plotting air and naval strategy; some dared to hope that the introduction of operations research would allow them an even broader hand in planning the landing.

Yranne, who had contributed so outstandingly to the first invention, was presently content with his lot, though another activity absorbed him as D-day approached. For several months he had been collecting a mass of reports from all sources, comparing, sifting, weighing them, and finally submitting them to the theory of probability. Almost certain now that the Alphas would win again, he backed this belief with sizable wagers. And since egoism was not in his nature, he decided to share the benefits of his knowledge with Zarratoff.

He found the astronomer sitting at his desk in a familiar posture of concentration, hunched over a map of the heavens showing various constellations. Apparently Zarratoff had returned to astronomy's fold after several months' absence and was pursuing his cosmic research. As usual, Yranne waited patiently for his friend to complete the calculations he was noting on a pad next to the map. Only when Zarratoff lifted his head, disclosing a peculiar gleam in his eye, did Yranne explain his visit and mention his prognostics.

"Now then, what tip are you bringing me?"

"The Alpha team. The probability is ninety-nine percent. You can stake all you've got on it."

"Thanks, it's done already because I knew it."

"You knew it?"

"I've made my own calculations and the conclusion I reached is no mere probability, overwhelming as that may be; it's a certainty."

"A certainty?"

"Absolute."

The astronomer snickered archly, and Yranne saw there was no use pressing him further. Nor did he try, for the fact that they had reached the same general conclusion was all that mattered.

Zarratoff brought out a bottle and the two drank to their success. They rejoiced on two accounts, for all their hopes were invested in the physics clan in addition to the anticipated return on their scholarly computations.

4

AFTER THE SHOCK of the first bombardment, interest shifted to the skies with the appearance of fighter planes. It came as a staggering blow to the Alpha camp of physicists to discover that enemy aircraft were nearly as numerous as their own, just as fast, and inflicting serious damage. Their astonishment sprang from two sources: First, it never occurred to them that biologists would be capable of turning out that large a quantity of operable machines in a single year; secondly, the remembrance of history had distorted their judgment once again, anchoring the conviction of their overwhelming air superiority in their minds with all the force of a scientific axiom. Betas had studied the same history lessons, but imagination prompted them to concentrate on fighter planes and antiaircraft artillery, with the result that soon the sky became streaked with the smoldering trails of downed bombers. This produced a whole new set of images for television to exploit with breathtaking effects.

About half past one, after exhaustively dramatizing those effects, the cameras shifted to another element of the struggle, a second air fleet heading inland at higher altitude. These were paratroopers, who shortly began descending in a calmer setting disturbed only by the distant rumble of bombs.

But another unpleasant surprise awaited the Alphas when their parachutists hovered only a hundred yards or so above the ground. A new theater of operations suddenly sprang out of the darkness, lit by the blinding glare of searchlights as machine guns opened a murderous target practice on men dangling helplessly from their cords.

"Treason!" shouted Yranne.

Evidently the Betas had been informed of the drop points, for this drama recurred wherever parachutists were descending, and the few reaching the ground met instant slaughter.

"Treason," echoed O'Kearn, glancing suspiciously at his colleague Sir Alex Keene.

"Treason," the latter agreed, with a faintly self-satisfied smirk.

Indeed the secret parachute operation had been betrayed to the defenders. A commentator appeared on the screen to explain this briefly, stressing that such tactics were perfectly acceptable. Unable to restrain their glee, Nobel physiologists burst into wild applause, drowning out the physicists' protests.

This preliminary stage of the landing continued longer than expected. With Beta fighter planes harassing the heavy bombers, coastal batteries kept pounding away, leaving the fleet in disarray and virtually paralyzed for most of the day while the Alpha high command, drawing on its reserves, sent up more planes — dive bombers this time — to wipe out enemy artillery.

They succeeded at the cost of heavy losses. Order returned to the convoy, enabling the Alphas to resume landing operations. But not until nightfall did the first troops finally put ashore, instead of earlier that morning according to their and history's plan. Such hazards merely added spice to the drama. Enthusiastic audiences hailed the fireworks of tracer bullets spewed into the night as machine guns opened fire from emplacements safely concealed from enemy bombers. Beta forces had mapped out a superb defense not to mention a whole series of surprises for the invaders. The latter suffered fresh losses but managed to gain a foothold, to advance, dig in, and finally unload light armored equipment followed by heavy tanks and artillery.

A furious battle erupted on the beaches of Normandy. Cameramen had all they could do to record the most vivid scenes: pairs of commandos struggling in the dark interspersed with sudden blasts of machine-gun fire and hand-to-hand knife assaults; flamethrowers incinerating machine-gun nests; artillery duels, tank attacks and counterattacks; infantry advancing on all fours to storm defense positions. For three straight days and nights the whole violent fantasy of the games unfolded nonstop in all its subtle shadings and startling contrasts before a spellbound world. Not for an instant were viewers bored, owing to the superb handling of the subject, the matchless staging, the conscious artistry guiding efforts to unify the production, and the desperate, valorous struggle of both teams for victory.

After three days of bitter fighting, however, the Beta cause began to founder. It seemed that despite the superhuman courage of their defenders, despite fearful losses inflicted on the enemy, the invaders had retained their foothold, reinforced their lines and equipment, and advanced. Cameras filmed several bridgeheads about to be consolidated, indicating that the Alphas were establishing a powerful, unbroken front from which to launch, probably, a decisive attack. In the amphitheater, with heads drooping mournfully, Nobel physiologists could not conceal their anguish. Only Sir Alex appeared blithe and serene.

His confidence, drawing on secret springs, never wavered. But just as the physics clan began crying victory and celebrating wildly, an astounding upset occurred, sending tremors of emotion around the world and totally reversing the situation in a matter of hours.

The first symptom was recorded by a cameraman filming a relatively tranquil scene inside an invasion pocket where Alphas were assembling a field gun that had been brought ashore in parts. One of them suddenly gripped his forehead, staggered, and fell dead without a shot being fired. Television viewers were just as mystified as his companions, who stood watching the writhing body as a second man collapsed in the same manner. Then a third, and on and on.

When a commentator urged them to be on the lookout for other such puzzling occurrences, camera crews began checking nearby troop clusters. The same thing was happening everywhere: Alphas were dropping like flies, singly, in twos, threes, fours, and in swarms. One whole company was wiped out in a matter of seconds.

"Treason!" O'Kearn was roaring now. "I recognize the hand of . . ."

The rest of his sentence dissolved in the uproar generated in the amphitheater by this senseless slaughter, but the scientist had been staring at his ever-smirking colleague Sir Alex Keene. Mrs. Han narrowed her lovely eyes in silent reflection.

The disease spread. It appeared on board of vessels now anchored close to shore and on landing craft delivering troops and equipment; it struck ordinary crewmen lining the decks as well as their star-studded superiors; it spared neither the sailors tending the winches nor the machinists below in the engine rooms.

This sudden death (for death it was: the victims stiffened after a series of convulsions, limbs rigid, eyes wide open in a glassy stare — an unmistakable posture) invaded the skies from which Alpha planes were plummeting right and left as their pilots succumbed.

The din of battle gradually diminished; dwindling ranks prevented Alphas from operating their weapons, and soon all gunfire ceased. A strange thing indeed, for Beta forces seemed to have been immunized against the mysterious disease. None of them had come down with it. Cameras showed them in high spirits, laughing and joking. Apparently they had been ordered to cease fire.

Absolute silence now reigned over the Alpha lines, over empty skies, over waters dotted with little boats bobbing aimlessly atop the waves, and over the land, where survivors stared dazedly at the carpet of twisted bodies. Silence also reigned in front of every television screen. The world trembled for an explanation. An announcer reported that an investigation was under way and the spectacle would be suspended until its findings were known.

5

THE INTERMISSION lasted nearly two hours. Breaks of this sort had been anticipated in case of a prolonged contest to let audiences relax while commentators reported the situation. Contestants were expected to stay put and not try to advance their positions until the game resumed. Both sides observed this rule, but Alphas kept collapsing and dying in horrible convulsions. The disease showed no mercy. To distract viewers, cameramen shot close-ups of the victims, all manifesting the same contorted limbs and limp, sagging flesh; all hollow-cheeked, blue-lipped, their eyes sunk deep beneath discolored ridges.

The investigation bore out suspicions fostered by those symptoms. And in any case the Betas made no attempt to hide the truth, for their commander himself came on the screen with an announcement dispelling all doubt.

Delighted at the unexpected occasion to put their expert knowledge to use, physicians, physiologists, bacteriologists, and other specialists of the biological sciences had carried out secret experiments on the cholera bacillus and succeeded in developing a highly virulent strain that killed like lightning.

"That's a dirty trick," Fawell shouted, shaking his fist at the figure on the screen as if it could hear him, "an unfair weapon, a discovery that didn't exist at the time of the landing and therefore against the rules of the game."

Sir Alex Keene, the famous bacteriologist, rose to answer him, exquisitely polite and sneering.

"Being a physicist, our learned and honorable President certainly may be excused for not knowing that the *vibrio cholerae* (I translate for his benefit: comma-shaped cholera bacillus) existed long before the landing. I permit myself to remind him, if he has forgotten it, or instruct him, if he does not know it, that Thucydides left us the description of a plague ravaging Athens in the fifth century B.C., a plague we biologists attribute with certainty to a manifestation of this bacillus. More recently, in the seventh century, a similar epidemic devastated India, as we have no reason to doubt from Susrata's account of the event. Now the rules of the game — with which you, Mr. President, cannot fail to be familiar — the rules of the game authorize contestants to *improve* any item existing during the period in question. We did precisely that. We —"

"We!" thundered O'Kearn. "You give yourself away."

"By 'we,' my dear colleague, I think you know I am referring to our valorous Beta defenders and the eminent experts assigned to aid them. As I was about to explain, they merely perfected this *vibrio* without recourse to any basic discovery of later date. Our scientists relied on patience and selection. I was kept informed of their work but did not intervene. So everything is fair and above board."

Fawell and every other physicist remained unconvinced. The President was on the verge of objecting when O'Kearn tapped him on the shoulder, motioning for silence. The great Nobel himself seemed pacified.

"But I tell you it's all his doing," Fawell protested. "The facts stare you in the face. It was his own field of research."

"I know," said O'Kearn.

"We ought to cancel the game and hold a serious inquiry. Physics had won. Umpires mustn't hand over the victory —"

"Calm yourself. There'd be no point in it. We'd never have proof."

"What shall we do then?"

"Be quiet and listen to me. I've suspected all along that he was cooking up a trick like this. . . ."

O'Kearn went on talking in a low voice. Fawell's outrage gradually dissolved into ripples of confusion scuttling across his brow. When the Nobel finished speaking, the world executive seemed to be wrestling with some strange dilemma. He opened his mouth as if to say something, then changed his mind.

"Anyway, there's nothing we can do," O'Kearn concluded. "We'll have to wait."

They returned to their seats in front of the television screen as the Beta leader was completing his statement. Smugly, he disclosed that at the very start of the game several bacteria-laden shells had sufficed to infect the beach area and a broad section of the ocean surface. After three days the disease struck, running its lightning course just as laboratory demonstrations had shown.

He assured his audience that there was no risk of a world epidemic as the danger zone had been rigidly contained. In any event biologists had developed a foolproof vaccine for total immunity, currently available in large quantities, another scientific achievement to their credit. The proof was that all Betas remained healthy, having been vaccinated before the game opened. Finally, he pointed out that umpires, cameramen, and television crews had survived because Beta doctors had vaccinated them on the sly, for humanitarian reasons and so as not to deprive viewers of the finale about to take place.

Now it was Yranne's turn to fly into a rage. His mounting nervousness dated from the first signs of an Alpha collapse. Evidently he had not foreseen this bacteriological innovation. With his probability projections founded on sand, he saw himself indebted for life by enormous betting losses. This time it was Zarratoff who tried to soothe his anger. Sitting beside him, the astronomer had show no sign of upset and seemed serenely confident of the game's outcome.

"Be quiet," he told Yranne. "Watch and listen. I'm certain the Alphas will win."

"How can you say that when they're dropping like flies every minute, every second, even during the intermission? They haven't a leg to stand on."

"I tell you it's an absolute certainty."

Betty Han in the next seat overheard this dialogue and stared at the astronomer with intense curiosity. Shrugging his shoulders in helpless rage, Yranne finally was silenced by his friend's unqualified assurance. Besides, it was too late to protest. They had just announced the investigation committee's report that no rule had been broken. There was no appeal; even the President was powerless to intervene. The game resumed.

6

THE CLIMAX approached, promising victory to biology's cause. Betas penetrating enemy-held pockets encountered no resistance; too disabled to defend themselves, the survivors were killed instantly. Betas then went about collecting bodies and dumping them into the sea, dead and wounded alike, taking no chances on having someone question their victory, the criterion of which was that no living Alpha must remain on Norman soil. This final cleanup operation lacked the color of the opening sequences. Not surprisingly, many viewers decided the spectacle was over and were preparing to desert the screen, carrying away enough exalting imagery to combat melancholy for months to come.

The drone of a motor changed their minds and lifted their eyes. At the first sound of it in the huge amphitheater, O'Kearn winked slyly at Fawell, who responded with a smile. Soon a plane appeared on the screen, a single aircraft, the last remnant of the Alpha fleet. It had been waiting in England, far from the fighting, for emergency use and now was bound for Norman shores. Beta defenders gaped at each other in astonishment. According to reports, the Alphas were not supposed to have a single piece of usable equipment left and were wholly resigned to defeat, too demoralized to even feign a hostile move. Anyway, the plane did not display the physics insignia as the rules required. Many people thought the craft was bringing umpires to declare a Beta victory and confer the palm on them.

They were wrong. Masters of the atom, masters of energy, the physicists could not accept such a humiliating defeat and were keeping one last decisive trump up their sleeve, even if using it meant stretching the rules of the game a bit. O'Kearn knew this and, suspecting some chicanery on the part of his rival Sir Alex Keene, had placed his scientific talents in the service of his clan by secretly collaborating in the manufacture of a bomb, a single one but more than powerful enough to reverse the situation all over again.

The Betas were annihilated along with dying Alphas. Unfortunately, viewers did not get to see the final holocaust, and for a moment their last image might have been the blinding flash following the bomb explosion, after which screens went blank.

In fact the physicists, who shared O'Kearn's view that Science must be independent of man and who lacked the biologists' concern for human existence, had forgotten to ensure the safety of television crews. Cameramen, umpires, and commentators were blown to bits in less than a second.

Not all of them, however. The lone survivor, a young cameraman, had been far enough from the point of impact and alert enough to leap into an underground shelter with all his equipment just before the blast. Instead of meeting instant death, he was able to climb out a few minutes later. Standing there burned, blinded, all but asphyxiated, and bombarded by swirling clouds of lethal particles, somehow he mustered the professional conscience to capture one last set of images and the instinct to turn his lens oceanward, focusing it on the sole filmworthy object.

Thanks to him, then, television audiences were not deprived of the momentous finale. Thanks to him, screens all over the world lit up again, transmitting a final vision in keeping with the whole unforgettable spectacle.

"Look!" exclaimed O'Kearn, clutching Fawell's shoulder. "We're winning!"

It was a tiny rubber boat with a single passenger struggling to row himself ashore. The figure turned out to be the Alpha commander; he and the cameraman were the sole survivors of the carnage. In his command post aboard the destroyer cruising fairly close to shore, he had managed to resist the cholera epidemic. The bomb and its deadly radiation also had spared him, but in the wake of swirling waters churned up by the cataclysm on land, on sea and in the air, an enormous ground swell buttressed by raging gusts of wind had suddenly propelled the warship coastward, causing it to founder and break up. Wasting no time, he lowered himself into the only boat available, a kind of miniature dinghy that somehow had weathered the tempest, and with every last ounce of fading strength, strained to reach those noxious, plague-ridden shores.

Grasping his purpose, television audiences stiffened in tense expectancy and solemn silence. Facing the screen in the great amphitheater, scientists and Nobels alike declared a truce in the violent quarrel lately erupted in their ranks. For a moment Sir Alex Keene stopped shaking his fist under O'Kearn's nose, and President Fawell, his own fist upraised, suddenly restrained himself from replanting it in the face of a biologist official who had come leaping at him with the cry: "Anthropocentrist!" The spectacle had reached its climax. All humanity was left paralyzed by this breathtakingly sublime ordeal of the dying Alpha commander. Would he make it?

He did. The cameraman, also in his death throes, filmed every last twitch. Lurching wildly, the commander succeeded in setting one unsteady foot after the other on shore. Standing there stiffly erect, on the verge of falling over dead, he raised both arms parallel toward the reeking sky in one last international salute symbolizing Science's eternal striving for progress as well as the final, indisputable victory of his clan. In fact victory demanded the presence of at least one living Alpha on the shore after total destruction of the enemy. This was indeed the case. The whole world was witness in the absence of vaporized umpires. The cause of physics triumphed according to the rules of the game.

In the wake of this emotional ordeal, and while Nobels resumed their wrangling and fighting, Yranne, mildly stunned, stood on the sidelines with Zarratoff, serene as ever, Betty Han, and Fawell, who had succeeded in disposing of his assailant. The mathematician mopped his forehead.

"My calculations were wrong," he said deliberately, "I'm the first to admit it, but they gave the right results. History and science abound in incidents of this sort; anyway, I won my bets."

"Now what I'd like to know, Zarratoff," Betty said, her narrowed eyes enveloping the astronomer in their piercing gaze, "is how you of all people could be certain of victory when the rest of us were on tenterhooks?"

"It's true," said Fawell, "I went on hoping after O'Kearn told me the secret, but you couldn't have known about this parting shot of ours that decided the game."

"I knew nothing about it," Zarratoff declared.

"What was it then?" his friends pressed him.

The astronomer smiled mysteriously. "You really want to know?"

They insisted; still smiling, he drew a slip of paper from his pocket and began unfolding it with the same air of mystery. He spread it out on a stand.

It was the map of the heavens Yranne had found him poring over and on which he was making calculations the day he wanted him to bet on the Alphas. It showed the sun and various planets linked by lines forming a diagram. The scientists in turn bent over the paper as they listened to the astronomer's explanation.

"I had consulted the heavens," he told them. "The date, the place, and the position of Mars and Mercury removed any doubt. An Alpha victory was guaranteed by the horoscope."